CHRISTOPHER BUSH
THE CASE OF THE GRAND ALLIANCE

CHRISTOPHER BUSH was born Charlie Christmas Bush in Norfolk in 1885. His father was a farm labourer and his mother a milliner. In the early years of his childhood he lived with his aunt and uncle in London before returning to Norfolk aged seven, later winning a scholarship to Thetford Grammar School.

As an adult, Bush worked as a schoolmaster for 27 years, pausing only to fight in World War One, until retiring aged 46 in 1931 to be a full-time novelist. His first novel featuring the eccentric Ludovic Travers was published in 1926, and was followed by 62 additional Travers mysteries. These are all to be republished by Dean Street Press.

Christopher Bush fought again in World War Two, and was elected a member of the prestigious Detection Club.

He died in 1973.

CHRISTOPHER BUSH

THE CASE OF THE GRAND ALLIANCE

With an introduction
by Curtis Evans

DEAN STREET PRESS

Published by Dean Street Press 2022

Copyright © 1964 Christopher Bush

Introduction copyright © 2022 Curtis Evans

All Rights Reserved

The right of Christopher Bush to be identified as the Author of the Work has been asserted by his estate in accordance with the Copyright, Designs and Patents Act 1988.

First published in 1964 by MacDonald & Co.

Cover by DSP

ISBN 978 1 915014 74 0

www.deanstreetpress.co.uk

For

EDWARD O'NEIL
(University of Southern California)

with gratitude

INTRODUCTION

Rosalind. If it be true that good wine needs no bush [i.e., advertising], 'tis true that a good play needs no epilogue. Yet to good wine, they do use good bushes, and good plays prove the better by the help of good epilogues.

–SHAKESPEARE, Epilogue, As You Like It

THE decade of the 1960s saw the sun finally begin to set on that storied generation which between the First and Second World Wars gave us detective fiction's Golden Age. Taking account of both deaths and retirements, by the late Sixties only a bare half-dozen pre-World War Two members of the Detection Club were still plying their deliciously deceptive craft: Agatha Christie, Anthony Gilbert (Lucy Beatrice Malleson), Gladys Mitchell, John Dickson Carr, Nicholas Blake and Christopher Bush, the subject of this introduction. Bush himself would pass away, at the age of eighty-seven, in 1973, having published, at the age of eighty-two, his sixty-third Ludovic Travers detective novel, *The Case of the Prodigal Daughter*, in the United Kingdom in the spring of 1968.

In the United States Bush's final detective novel did not appear until late November 1969, about four months after the horrific Manson murders in the tarnished Golden State of California. Implicating the triple terrors of sex, drugs and rock and roll (not to mention almost inconceivably bestial violence), the Manson slayings could not have strayed farther from the whimsically escapist "death as a game" aesthetic of Golden Age of detective fiction. Increasingly in the decade capable of producing psychedelic psychopaths like Charles Manson and his "family," the few remaining survivors of the Golden Age of detective fiction increasingly deemed themselves men and women far out of time. In his detective fiction John Dickson Carr, an incurable romantic, prudently beat a retreat from the present into the pleasanter pages of the past, setting his tales in bygone historical eras where he felt vastly more at home. With varying success Agatha Christie made a brave effort to stay abreast of the times (*Third Girl*, *Endless Night*), but ultimately her strivings to understand what was going on around her collapsed into the utter incoherence of *Passenger to Frankfurt* and *Postern of Fate*, by general consensus the worst mystery novels that Dame Agatha ever put down on paper.

In his detective fiction Christopher Bush, who was not quite two years older than Christie, managed rather better than the Queen of Crime to keep up with all the unsettling goings-on around him, while never forswearing the Golden Age article of faith that the primary purpose of a crime writer is pleasingly to puzzle his/her readers. And, in contrast with Christie and Carr, Bush knew when it was time to lay down his pen (or turn off his dictation machine, as the case may be), thereby allowing him to make his exit from the stage on a comparatively high note. Indeed, Christopher Bush's concluding baker's dozen of detective novels, which he published between 1957 and 1968 (and which have now been reprinted, after more than a half-century, by Dean Street Press), makes a generally fine epilogue, or coda, to the author's impressive corpus of crime fiction, which first began to see the light of day way back in the jubilant Jazz Age. These are, readers will find, "good bushes" (to punningly borrow from Shakespeare), providing them with ample intelligent detective entertainment as Bush's longtime series sleuth Ludovic Travers, in the luminous twilight of his career, makes his final forays into ingenious criminal investigation.

*

In the last thirteen Ludovic Travers mystery novels, Travers' *entrée* to his cases continues to come through his ownership of the Broad Street Detective Agency. Besides Travers we also regularly encounter his elegant wife, Bernice (although sometimes his independent-minded spouse is away on excursions of her own), his proverbially loyal secretary, Bertha Munney, his top Broad Street op, Hallows (another one named French, presumably inspired by Bush's late Detection Club colleague Freeman Wills Crofts, pops up occasionally), John Hill of the United Assurance Agency, who brings Travers many of his cases, and Scotland Yard's Inspector Jewle and Sergeant Matthews, who after the first of these final novels, *The Case of the Treble Twist* (in the U.S. *Triple Twist*), are promoted, respectively, to Superintendent and Inspector. (The Yard's ex-Superintendent George Wharton, now firmly retired from any form of investigative work whatsoever, is mentioned just once by Ludo, when, in *The Case of the Dead Man Gone*, he passingly imparts that he and Wharton recently had lunch together.)

For all practical purposes Travers, who during the Golden Age was a classic gentleman amateur snooper like Philo Vance and Lord Peter Wimsey, now functions fully as a professional private eye—although one, to be sure, who is rather posher than the rest. While some reviewers referred to Travers as England's Philip Marlowe, in fact he little resembles the general run of love and leave 'em/hate and beat 'em brand of brutish American P.I.'s, favoring a nice cup of coffee (a post-war change from tea), a good pipe and the occasional spot of sherry to the frequent snatches of liquor and cigarettes favored by most of his American brethren and remaining faithful to his spouse despite encountering a succession of sexy women, not all of them, shall we say, virtuously inclined.

This was a formula which throughout the period maintained a devoted audience on both sides of the Atlantic consisting, one surmises, of readers (including crime writers Anthony Berkeley, Nicholas Blake and the late Alan Hunter, creator of Inspector George Gently) who preferred their detectives something less than hard-boiled. Travers himself sneers at the hugely popular (and psychotically violent) postwar American private eye Mike

Hammer, commenting of an American couple in *The Case of the Treble Twist*: "She was a woman of considerable culture; his ran about as far as Mickey Spillane" [a withering reference to Mike Hammer's creator]. Yet despite his manifest disdain for Mike Hammer, an ugly American if ever there were one, Christopher Bush and his wife Florence in the spring of 1957 had traveled to New York aboard the RMS *Queen Elizabeth*, and references by him to both the United States and Canada became more frequent in the books which followed this trip.

Certainly *The Case of the Treble Twist* (1957) features tough customers and an exceptionally cruel murder, yet it is also one of Bush's most ingeniously contrived cases from the Fifties, full of charm, treacherous deception and, yes, plenty of twists, including one that is a real sockaroo (to borrow, as Bush occasionally did, from American idiom). Similarly clever is *The Case of the Running Man* (1958), which draws, as several earlier Bush books had, on the author's profound love and knowledge of antiques. By this time Bush and his wife, their coffers having burgeoned from the proceeds of his successful mysteries, resided in the quaint medieval market town of Lavenham, Suffolk at the Great House, a splendidly decorated fourteenth-century structure with an elegant Georgian-era façade which he and Florence purchased in 1953 and resided in until their deaths. The dashing author, whom in 1967 *Chicago Tribune* mystery reviewer Alice Crombie swooningly dubbed "one of the handsomest mystery writers on either side of the Channel or Atlantic," also drove a Jaguar, beloved by James Bond films of late, well into his eighties.

The Case of the Running Man includes that Golden Age detective fiction staple, a family tree, but more originally the novel features as a major character a black American man, Sam, the devoted chauffeur of the wealthy murder victim. Sam, who reminds Ludovic Travers of Rochester, "Jack Benny's factotum of television and radio," is an interesting and sincerely treated individual, although as Anthony Boucher amusingly pronounced at the time in the *New York Times Book Review*, he speaks "a dialect never heard by mortal ear"—an odd compounding of "American Negro" and London cockney.

The Case of the Careless Thief (1959) takes Ludo to Sandbeach, "the Blackpool of the South Coast," as the American jacket blurb puts it, with "a dozen hotels, a race track, a dog track, a music hall and two enormous dance halls." Anthony Boucher deemed this hard-hitting, tricky tale, which draws to strong effect on contemporary events in England, "one of Ludovic Travers' best cases." Likewise hard-hitting are *The Case of the Sapphire Brooch* (1960) and *The Case of the Extra Grave* (1961), complex tales of murderous mésalliances with memorably grim conclusions. The plot of *The Case of the Dead Man Gone* (1961) topically involves refugee relief groups, while *The Case of the Heavenly Twin* (1963) opens with a case of a creative criminal couple forging American Express Travelers Checks, concerning which Americans of a certain age will recall actor Karl Malden sternly enjoining, in a long-running television advertising campaign: "Don't leave home without them." In contrast with many of his crime writing contemporaries (judging from the tone of their work), Bush actually learned to watch and enjoy television, although in *The Case of The Three-Ring Puzzle*, a tale of violently escalating intrigue, Travers dryly references Scottish philosopher Thomas Carlyle's famous observation that England's population consisted of "mostly fools" when he comments: "I guess he wasn't too far out at that. But rather remarkable an estimate perhaps, considering that in his day there were no television commercials."

Of Bush's final five Ludovic Travers detective novels, published between 1964 and 1968, when the Western World, in the eyes of many, was going from whimsically mod to utterly mad, the best are, in my estimation, the cases of *The Jumbo Sandwich* (1965), *The Good Employer* (1966) and

The Prodigal Daughter (1968). In *Sandwich* a crisp case of a defrauded (and jilted) gentry lady friend of Ludo's metamorphoses into a smorgasbord of, as the American book jacket puts it, "blackmail, black magic, a black sheep, and murder." It all culminates in a confrontation on a lonely Riviera beach in France, setting of some of Ludovic Travers' earliest cases, between Ludo and a desperate killer, in which Bernice plays an unexpectedly active part. Ludo again travels to France in the highly classic *Employer*, which draws most engagingly on the sleuth's (and the author's) dabbling in the world of art and is dedicated to his distinguished Lavenham artist friends, the couple Reginald and Rosalie Brill, who resided next door to Bush and his wife at the fourteenth-century Little Hall, then an art student hostel for which the Brills served as guardians. In *The Guardian* Francis Iles (aka Golden Age crime writer Anthony Berkeley) pronounced that *Employer* represented Bush "at his most ingenious."

Finally, in *Daughter* Travers finds himself tasked with recovering the absconded teenage offspring of domineering Dora Marport, sober-sided head of the organization Home and Family, which is righteously devoted to "the fostering, so to speak, of family life as the stoutest bulwark against the encroachment of ever-more numerous hostile forces: sex and violence in literature, films and on television; pornography generally, and the erosion of responsibility and the capability for sacrifice by the welfare state." Can Travers, a Great War veteran who made his debut in detective fiction in 1926, bridge the generation gap in late-Sixties London? Ludo may prefer Bach to the Beatles, but in this, the last of his recorded cases, he proves more "with it" than one might have expected. All in all, *Daughter* makes a rewarding finish to one of the longest-running and most noteworthy sleuth series in British detective fiction.

Curtis Evans

1

EVA STRAND

It was four years ago, in 1959, that we at the Broad Street Detective Agency became involved in the tragic affair of Eva Strand. She didn't call by appointment. Bertha Munney, our secretary-receptionist, rang through at about half-past eleven one June morning to say that a Mrs. Eva Strand would like to see me personally, and professionally. She added that the matter about which Mrs. Strand wanted to see me was reasonably urgent. That last phrase is a kind of code we use. Since Bertha is speaking in the presence of a prospective client, there has to be some kind of private arrangement to give me in my room an idea of both business and client. What Bertha had told me over the inter-com. was that I ought to see Mrs. Strand and that the said Mrs. Strand was perturbed but not unduly so.

So Bertha showed the lady into my room. A lady, by the generally accepted meaning, she definitely was. She was in the late forties, tallish, very spare and perfectly assured. Flecks of greying hair showed at the edges of the beehive hat. In her younger days she must have been someone at whom one turned to look: now there was still a distinction, though the face was pale and the dark eyes a bit sunken.

"Mrs. Strand?" I said, and smiled as I took over from Bertha.

"Yes," she said. "And you're Mr. Travers?"

"Yes, Mrs. Strand. But won't you sit down?"

But she didn't take at once the chair I moved for her. "The Mr. Travers who knows my husband?"

Her name wasn't all that common and I didn't have to think very long. Martin Strand was a member of my club and I had served with him recently on a committee. We weren't in any way friends: just the usual club acquaintances who nod and smile at each other across a dining table or wave a quiet hand in the reading room. I did have quite a respect for him.

He was in fact the kind of man whom one regrets not to have known much earlier and much better.

I got Eva Strand seated, and almost at once I began to notice the small signs of perturbation that Bertha had spotted. The gloved hands were fidgeting with the handbag and she was giving quick, almost furtive looks around the room.

"A cigarette, Mrs. Strand?" I gave my best smile as I offered her the box.

"Thank you, no," she said. "I was smoking far too much and had to give it up."

"Very brave of you. I generally smoke a pipe. If I remember rightly, your husband smokes a pipe too."

"Yes," she said. "But about Martin, Mr. Travers. He's on no account to know that I've been here to see you."

"Nobody will know," I assured her. "If you're here on your own confidential business, no one will ever know that you've been here."

"You definitely promise that?"

"I give you my personal word. If you're here to ask us to make, say, confidential enquiries, even the one who makes those enquiries will be as far as possible ignorant of the identity—even the sex—of the person for whom he's working."

I produced my best smile again. "Does that reassure you?"

"Thank you."

She said it quietly. There was even a little smile, and the restless fingers were all at once still.

"There are two things I ought to add," I went on. "We never on any account handle domestic problems—divorce and that kind of thing. I take it yours is not that sort of problem?"

"Oh, no. Nothing like that. All I want you to do is find someone for me."

"Then we'll certainly try to do just that," I told her. "But there is one other thing. I may not be able to undertake the enquiry personally, but whoever does handle it will be someone to be implicitly trusted. I tell you that because it may help him and the enquiry if he knows your name. But we'll come to that later. Suppose you tell me just what we have to do."

I tell it to you in a somewhat roundabout way. I didn't know Martin Strand's financial position but I was pretty sure he was a reasonably wealthy man. He was chairman of Strandway Foods Limited, a large concern with branches in various parts of the world. When I later checked in the *Financial Times* I saw that the five-shilling shares of the company stood at just over eleven shillings.

Eva Strand's information about herself was given in what I can only call a very grudging way. During the war she was for a time in Norwich and there she met some people called Rawson who were extremely kind to her. In 1943, while she was there, a daughter, Ruth, was born to the Rawsons. Soon afterwards Eva left Norwich and in 1945 she married Martin Strand. His father was then chairman of the company and Martin, a junior director, spent his honeymoon in Vancouver where there was business to do with one of the company's branches.

When the young married couple returned to England in the early summer of 1946, Eva Strand tried to get into touch with the Rawsons but without success. She was of the opinion that they had left Norwich. A year or two later, when her husband was on a flying visit to Bombay, she had visited Norwich herself. She didn't tell me what actual enquiries she had made but she assured me that the Rawsons were then no longer in the city, nor had they left any clear traces she could follow.

"We have to start somewhere," I said, "so what was the Rawsons' address when you knew them?"

She gave that quick, nervous clutching of the bag again. "I don't really know. I forget. I remember it was in that wide road as you come in from London."

"The Newmarket Road? Large Victorian houses well spaced? A lot of trees?"

"Yes. That's the road. About half-way along. I'm almost sure. A Georgian kind of house with a slate roof. On the right-hand side when you're coming from the city. I forget the actual name. If it had one. I could always walk straight to it when I went there."

"And did you find it when you last went to Norwich again?"

"No. Everything seemed to have changed. Everything changes so, you know."

"That's only too true," I told her consolingly. "But the Rawsons themselves. What were their names?"

"Will—maybe William but she always called him Will. She was Janice."

"And what was Will Rawson's business of profession?"

"I really don't know—not for certain. I believe he had some-thing to do with farming."

I gave a quick, incredulous smile. I think I flashed it off my face before she really noticed it.

"How old a man was he?"

"In the thirties: the early thirties."

"Then his farming interests might mean that he was a repre-sentative for a fertiliser or machinery company?"

"Yes," she said, and a bit too quickly. "I seem to remember it was something like that."

I asked some other questions: some direct and others from concealed angles, but little else emerged that seemed worth while. And there you may assume that the interview was at an end except for a few oddments. Let me give them categorically so that you can see what you can make of them.

a. The Strands had an apartment at Knowland House, Lancaster Gate, but I was not to report to her there by letter. I was to ring her only between eleven and twelve in the morning.

b. When I mentioned our terms, she agreed at once. She waved aside the retainer of fifty pounds and insisted on handing me two hundred pounds. She produced the notes from her bag.

c. She was insistent once more on the absolutely confidential nature of the case. She again specifically mentioned her husband.

d. She added, as a kind of afterthought, a little more about the sixteen-year-old Ruth Rawson who was the one we were actually to find. Why she wanted to get into touch was that since she couldn't do anything to repay the kindnesses all those years ago of the Rawsons, she could at least leave a substantial legacy to the daughter, Ruth—if she were still living.

When Bertha escorted Mrs. Strand out—I'd left her with a reassuring handshake at my door—I lighted my pipe and did some thinking. I doubt, in fact, if ever an embryo of a case had ever given me such an uneasiness as I then had. I may not have conveyed it to you but Eva Strand had not looked unwell but had acted generally as someone under a considerable strain. Maybe that had affected her memory.

I harked back in my mind to those war-time years and found myself remembering well enough, and yet there had been things said now to be forgotten which she should easily have remembered. I refer to the Rawsons generally. There had been not only half-truths, but also evasions, and there had been at least one thing that seemed untrue. I'm an East Anglian and I know Norwich like the back of my hand. Eva Strand hadn't known that, and I hadn't chosen even to hint at it, so when she had said that things had changed a lot in the Newmarket Road since 1943 she had been very, very wrong. That road is still virtually as I remembered it from my boyhood. I knew, because I had driven along it only a few months before.

Then there had been that over-and-over again insistence on everything being kept from her husband. But why? In heaven's name, why? She had been befriended years ago by kindly people and now she wanted to repay by leaving a legacy to their daughter. Then why on earth shouldn't her husband be told those simple facts? I couldn't conceive of a man like Martin Strand making any objection.

What I finally decided was to make a few discreet enquiries, and I'd begin by lunching at the club. Strangely enough, all my doubts and apprehensions disappeared as soon as I'd had a word with Harry Burstall, the secretary.

"Has Martin Strand been along lately? I don't seem to have seen him."

"He hasn't been in for quite a time," he said. "That business of his daughter was quite a shock to him."

"What business was that?"

"Meningitis. Dead inside a week. His only daughter. The only child, in fact. I believe it affected his wife pretty badly too."

"Must have been a terrible shock," I said. "Recently, was it?"

"About three months ago."

I said I was very sorry. I had both a liking and a respect for Martin Strand and now it was too late to offer condolences. But the news did clear my mind. It explained all sorts of things. Why Eva Strand had still looked so unwell, for instance. And why the loss of her only child had turned her thoughts to someone else's daughter and had created the wish to bring happiness to that daughter. And why her memory had been so faulty. And even why she had been so insistent on keeping everything from her husband. What she would be doing in leaving a legacy to Ruth Rawson was something which would not be known till after her own death. To mention it now to her husband might be to revive the tragedy for him.

In fact my mind was now absolutely at rest. All that remained was to get on with the case. That's why I rang Tom Jordan's Agency—London Enquiries.

There are three of us who work at times together, lending so to speak, a helping hand. All are reputable agencies and Tom Jordan's is much larger than my own, though I doubt if his turnover is much greater. He handles all sorts of work, including divorce, and that requires a large staff. Most of our work is contract business for a couple of insurance companies and a sprinkling of large business firms.

My problem was that at the moment things were happening all at once and we just didn't have the right kind of man available for the Ruth Rawson enquiry, nor was I available myself. The one man for the job would have been Bob Hallows. He was then our senior operative, but recently he's become a director. I'd have liked to transfer him to the Ruth Rawson case, but it was something that just couldn't be done. That was why, after lunch, I called on Tom Jordan. I've known him for a good many years. He's now in the early sixties.

If there's to be an association between agencies, there's also to be implicit confidence. Maybe that's why there're only three of us, and why it's taken the experience of years to form the kind of association that now exists. My promise to Eva Strand, then, didn't include Tom Jordan. He's me in a case like this—if you know what I mean—and I'm him. That may be bad grammar but it's damn-good sense. If I lend a man to Tom, I want to know what it's all about—and I mean all, not part. Then I decide if to lend a man and what kind of man. If anything goes wrong—and, believe me, in our business, things do go wrong—then the responsibility is as much mine as his.

"Sounds a pretty straightforward case," he said, "but you'll need a man with a bit of class. A good mixer."

"You've someone in mind?"

"Maybe," he said. "I'm pretty sure you haven't met him. His name's Templett. Geoff Templett. Single. Just over thirty. Good-looking young chap. Quite well-educated and pretty smart generally."

"Sounds just the man. He's handy?"

"Not at the moment. I can have him at Broad Street at nine in the morning, though."

So at nine the next morning I was interviewing Geoff Templett. I liked the look of him. He was just under six feet: lithe with it, dark-haired and with a mobile, intelligent face. He spoke quite well and he was a good listener. If he asked a question, it was to the point.

"As I said at the start, there isn't a great deal to go on," I told him as I finally handed over the typed sheet of the tenuous clues we had. "Still, I've no doubt you'll ferret out a lot more. As soon as you know the whereabouts of this Ruth Rawson, and have enough particulars so that she can be properly named as a legatee in a will, then you'll have finished the job. You've got that?"

"Yes, sir. I make sure she's alive and the daughter of this Will and Janice Rawson, and where she is and what she's actually doing at the moment."

"Exactly. I don't need to tell you that everything has to be done circumspectly. You don't mind if I suggest something?"

"Why not, sir?"

"You were thinking of beginning at Norwich?"

"Well it was in my mind."

"Then do something else first. See the marriage certificate of Will and Janice Rawson at Somerset House, and the daughter's birth certificate. There might be something that gives you ideas."

I held out my hand as he rose to go.

"No need to report till you have something. Or think you could do with some extra help. I shan't bother you. The job's your own from now on. Be discreet and don't be afraid of spending money if you think it'll produce results."

That was about all. We'd already been over possible clues and likely forms of attack, and that mention of discretion had referred to any advertising in the local press. He'd seemed receptive enough, and as soon as I'd fixed him up financially, he left. I was satisfied that Tom Jordan had sent me the right man for the job, and I rang him and told him so. After that there was nothing to do but get on with other business in hand and wait patiently for results.

Three days later, Templett rang me in the early afternoon. "Nothing doing so far, sir. Everything went wrong from the start."

"How do you mean? Something at Somerset House?"

"No, sir: that was all right. It was when I got here and began going through the directories and the electoral rolls. I also went through the casualty lists of the big air-raid, though that might have been earlier and I couldn't find that anyone of the name of Rawson had ever lived in Newmarket Road."

"That's extraordinary," I said. "The client was most clear about it."

"Well, I'm sorry, sir, but that's how it is. I did find two other lots of Rawsons but there was not the least connection. Also I've had an Urgently Wanted advert, in the local paper but with no results as yet."

"It's still early," I told him. "Go on doing all you can. Give me a ring in two or three days' time."

If it had been the late morning I think I'd have rung Eva Strand. But it wasn't, and then a minute or two's thought told me I'd have been very wrong. Maybe she was still mentally ill. What she had recently seen through the mind's eye of the events of sixteen years before had been through a clouded glass. Newmarket Road had been queerly confused with some other road, just as the Will Rawson had been vaguely connected with farming, and just as I had had to prompt her over and over again to get something of a description of the Rawsons as they'd been in 1943.

When Templett rang me again it was only to say there was still no news. I told him to insert an advertisement in the principal dailies of Suffolk, Cambridgeshire and Lincoln, just in case the Rawsons had moved that far away. As it was still well short of noon I rang Eva Strand. There was no reply. I waited a few moments and rang again. I could hear the bell shrilling but there was obviously nobody in the flat.

Templett rang at the end of the week. There had been no reply to any of the advertisements. To go on, he suggested, would be a waste of time and money. He had checked and rechecked every possible source of information and, as far as results were concerned, the Rawsons had either never existed or had disappeared without trace.

"Perhaps you're right," I told him. "It isn't the disappearance that worries me so much as the fact that as far as Norwich is concerned, they don't seem ever to have existed."

It was again well short of midday, so I rang Eva Strand. This time she answered.

"This is Ludovic Travers, Mrs. Strand. So sorry I haven't been able to give you any news, but, believe me, we've been doing everything we possibly can. We just can't pick up the trail of the Rawsons in Norwich. As far as our enquiries go, they might never have existed."

"Don't lie to me!"

The words came so explosively that the receiver almost left my hand.

"God may forgive you for what you've done to me but I never shall. I only wish I could make you suffer as you've made me suffer."

I hardly remember what I stammered out. Perhaps I said that I didn't understand. I'd done nothing to her except follow her instructions: admittedly with no results as yet, but that was no fault of mine. Then I realised I was babbling into a dead phone.

I let out a breath as I leaned back in my chair. For a moment I was furiously angry. Who did the woman think I was? God? I'd promised nothing, except to do my best. The fee hadn't been dependent on results. As for making her suffer by not producing a missing person from a conjurer's hat, that was sheer hysteria.

The thought pulled me suddenly up. The quality of her voice: everything she had said. Hysteria: nothing but hysteria. Eva Strand was mentally sick. To my mind there was all at once no doubt about it. Before I knew it, the anger had become a kind of shame. Maybe the fault was my own, or was I being sorry after the event? Perhaps I should never have taken the case. The turgidity of her memory, the hesitations, and the readiness to accept suggestions and ideas which I had been forced to put almost into her mouth: all that should have made me find excuses to usher her tactfully out of my office.

Some twinge of conscience made me lunch at the club. I think I was hoping to see Strand there and to find some excuse for a brief chat. Then, in the afternoon, Templett came back. After we'd gone over everything again and I'd settled his accounts, he asked if there was anything else, as he rose to go. I wondered why he was shaking his head.

"If you don't mind me saying so, Mr. Travers, I'm not very happy about all this. I don't think I've come out of it very well."

"What utter nonsense!" I told him. "If blame has to be attached to anyone, I'm the one who couldn't find you enough ideas to work on. You did everything I asked you to do."

He didn't speak for a moment and then he asked if he might say something.

"I think this business may have done me a lot of good. You see, I was beginning to think I was pretty good at my job. I don't mind telling you I was a bit ambitious. I'd even thought of setting up an agency of my own some day. What I know now is I've the hell of a lot still to learn."

"Haven't we all?" I told him. "No need to make yourself any kind of martyr. I'm satisfied and Mr. Jordan will be satisfied. That ought to be enough to reassure you."

Later that afternoon Hallows reported back at the office and, because maybe I wanted to ease my mind, I had quite a talk with him about that abortive case. There's nothing obsequious about Hallows. When he gave it as his considered opinion that we'd done our best, it was pretty good hearing.

"As for that business over the telephone, she must have been a bit unhinged. Also she'd expected too much."

"All the same, I'd like you to have a shot at the case yourself," I said. "Start absolutely from scratch. See me in the morning and we'll go over everything that's happened so far. If finding that girl is going to make Mrs. Strand any better mentally, then I think we're under an obligation to have another shot at it."

But we didn't. When I arrived at Broad Street in the morning, Hallows was waiting for me. He gave me a newspaper, finger on a marked paragraph. "I don't know if you've seen this."

I hadn't seen it. That's why it came as such a shock.

WOMAN FALLS FROM WINDOW OF FLAT
DOCTOR SAYS KILLED INSTANTLY

Shortly before six o'clock last night a Mrs. Martin Strand fell from a third storey window of her flat at Knowland House, Lancaster Gate. Death was instantaneous.
It is understood that the deceased has recently been in poor health. Some months ago she suffered a severe shock through the death of her daughter. The Police say there is no suspicion whatever of foul play.

So that was that. As far as I was concerned, wisdom had been justified of her children. The tragedy was that even the glimmerings of wisdom had come far too late. Now there was nothing whatever that I could do.

Mrs. Strand had come to me in strict confidence: if not, I might have confessed to Martin Strand that I might have contributed in some guiltless way to his wife's death. Nor was there any money to hand over to the estate. Templett's expenses came pretty heavy and there'd been the commission to Tom Jordan.

I did follow closely the proceedings at the inquest, admittedly because I feared that near her end Eva Strand might have said something to her husband about the visit to the Broad Street Detective Agency and its reasons. But nothing of that nature emerged. There was only one surprise.

After Martin Strand had mentioned the tragic death of their only child, he was asked if there was anything else which might have contributed to his wife's acute depression.

"There was what we thought was a possible burglary attempt at our apartment," he said. "One morning just over a week ago a man called at the apartment and said he had to check the telephone. My wife took him at his face value—I mean he looked the part—and let him in. He went through the motions of working at the telephone and left after about ten minutes. My wife told me about it when I got home that late afternoon and I guessed there was something wrong so I got into touch with the House Exchange, who knew nothing about it, and then informed the police. They discovered the man had not been sent by the telephone authority."

When asked if the man had taken anything, Strand said the only thing missing was a silver frame in which was a photograph of himself and his wife taken many years before. On their honeymoon in fact But the whole affair, trivial as it was, had upset his wife very much. The following morning he had made arrangements to take a three months' cruise round the world. Her doctor had agreed that it was the best possible thing that could be done to lift her out of her depression.

That was virtually all and, as far as I was concerned, the whole case was slowly forgotten. About three months later I ran across Tom Jordan and I asked him about Templett.

"He's no longer with us. Didn't you know? He left us about a fortnight after he did that job for you."

"News to me," I said. "Did he give any reasons?"

"A whole lot of garbled stuff. Said he didn't feel he'd made a good job of what he'd done for you and thought he ought to have new experience. Said he might go to the States where he had relations, and try his hand in an agency out there."

That was the last I thought I'd ever hear of Geoff Templett. Maybe I said as much to Jordan: I don't know. If I did, I was being dogmatic out of turn. I thought it if I didn't say it: which proves in any case how wrong one can sometimes be.

2

THE CREWE JEWELS

OUR principal source of income is undoubtedly United Assurance: Headquarters, Lombard Street: managing director, John Hill. As far as we are concerned, United Assurance have priority, and when John Hill wants us really urgently, we drop everything we can and get to Lombard Street at the double. One such occasion arose on Tuesday the 5th of November: Guy Fawkes Day is a good reminder if you ever want to hark back to it.

In the course of the enquiry which arose out of that Tuesday morning session at Lombard Street, we had to meet a number of people, and since it takes quite a time to sort people out and get them definitely fixed in one's mind, I'm going to hold up the progress of the drama to make you very briefly acquainted with some of those concerned. The following scant biographies should enable you to have at the back of your mind some basic facts about some of them before you actually meet them. There are two, however, whom you will never meet. Both are dead.

Sir Morton Crewe died in 1960 at the age of 80. His wife died in the October of this year, 1963, at the age of seventy-six.

SIR MORTON CREWE. One of the early pioneers of British aviation. Founded Crewe Aircraft Limited. After his death the firm was acquired by one of the big combines as a subsidiary. The Crewes lived at Pentlow House, Newhurst, Bucks., which was handy for the company's works at Watford. They also had a smaller house—Southways, Hollindale, Bucks. Sir Morton had been a founder member of what was to become the famous Hollindale golf course. He played there—golf was his only hobby—whenever he could spare the time. In his will he left that smaller house to his wife's nephew, Alan Cofield.

LADY (LAURA) CREWE. One of those notable pilots who emerged during and immediately after the 1914-18 war. Whereas her husband was a self-made man, she came from a very old north-country family with a long history of military and political service. Laura was the only daughter. Her brother was killed in 1917, leaving a baby son, the Alan Cofield already mentioned. Already mentioned also is the fact that she died about a month before that Lombard Street meeting.

So much for the dead; now for the living.

DAVID CREWE. Only child of Morton and Laura Crewe. Educated Harrow and Balliol. In early manhood became tubercular, and after recovery acquired a farm in the Kenya Highlands where the climate would be beneficial to his health.

JULIA CREWE. Wife of David Crewe. No children. She was the daughter of early Kenya settlers, and David had met her when she was studying at Lady Margaret Hall.

ALAN COFIELD. In addition to the bare facts already given, it should be added that his uncle had expected him ultimately to join the management of Crewe Airways, but at Watford he never contrived to settle down. He soon developed into a sort of general amanuensis at Pentlow House and, after his uncle's death, hovered between his own newly inherited house and Pentlow House, where he became indispensable to his aunt. He was a scratch golfer who had more than once survived a few rounds in the Amateur Championship.

And so to that morning of 5th November, 1963. As soon as I arrived at Broad Street and Norris, our general manager, had told me that John Hill had already rung the office, I guessed that something urgent must be in the wind. Hill rarely reaches his own office before half-past nine.

"He didn't seem inclined to tell me what it was all about," Norris said, "but he wanted you to call him as soon as you got in."

So I rang United Assurance. Hill was on the line before I'd hardly had time to settle the receiver to my ear.

"Glad you were early," he said. "Something rather unusual has cropped up here and I'd like you and Bob Hallows to see me here in the course of the next half-hour."

"We're all working directors here," I told him. "Hallows was working late last night and he's not due in yet. Still, I'll do what I can."

"Do your best," he said. "Some people immediately concerned in the matter are coming in at eleven this morning and it's urgent that you should be absolutely conversant with what's happened."

Hallows had already finished breakfast and thought he could just about manage Lombard Street in half an hour. John Hill has a special affection for Hallows. Most of Hallows's cases used to be concerned with arson or similar trickeries by which the clever ones hope to enrich themselves at the expense of insurance companies. Hill wasn't the only one who had a respect for Hallows. He's been in the detective game all his life, and those who've worked with him wouldn't hesitate to vote him the best in town. He has that rare quality of being able to melt into a background—any background—and unobtrusiveness is only one of his qualities. He's always unruffled: he's tenacious, extraordinarily perceptive, and years of varied experience have given him an intuition that at times seems almost clairvoyance.

He and I were only a few minutes late when we stepped into John Hill's office. It was still short of ten o'clock, but we didn't refuse the offer of coffee. Hill likes our conferences to be informal. He thinks it helps and maybe he's right.

"I'll go over this business slowly," he told us, "so that you can make appropriate notes. First, the people who're going to be here later this morning: just about an hour's time. There'll be a Mrs. Julia Crew and her husband's cousin Alan Cofield: also a Mr. Stephen Daunt who's the present head of John Parwell, the Saffron Row jewellers. You've heard of them?"

I said I definitely had. I'd never seen the actual premises since Saffron Row is quite a bit off Old Bond Street, but I'd seen the name of Parwell often enough. I'm not a collector nowadays—prices have soared well above me—but I still subscribe by way of academic interest to the marked catalogues of both Sotheby's and Christie's and there the name of Parwell was always turning up in old silver and jewellery. There are plenty of such old-established, unobtrusive firms in the Bond Street area. A look at their premises might give you the idea that bankruptcy was just around the corner, whereas their annual turnover must be well into six figures. The list of wealthy collectors on their books is longer than my pretty long arm.

"Old John Parwell died about a month ago," Hill went on. "The business was left to his nephew, Stephen Daunt. Daunt married the step-daughter about a year ago. I gather he's very much older than his wife, not that that's particularly relevant. Daunt was in charge of the firm's only branch, in Edinburgh, and I gather that he still has to go up there though, of course, he's taken over here. But he wasn't at Edinburgh on Saturday morning last, which is what matters. He was here in London. You've got the hang of all that?"

We said we had.

"Now to the clients," Hill went on. "I think you'll remember the name of Sir Morton Crewe who founded Crewe Aircraft. He was a very well-known figure. His widow died about a month ago and her only son and his wife flew from Kenya for the funeral. The son's very much of an invalid: chest always weak and now quite bad arthritis: so Julia Crewe—the daughter-in-law—had quite a lot of business on her hands what with settling the estate and disposing of things generally. They're returning as soon as possible to Kenya, where they've lived for a good many years. Apparently she's been helped quite a lot by an Alan Cofield, the late Sir Morton's nephew by marriage, who always seems to have been a kind of son of the house. Pentlow House, by the way, that's at Newhurst, Bucks., not far from Chesham. I'm afraid that's a bit garbled, but you'll fit it all in much better when we get to the real business in hand. And that's this.

"The late Lady Crewe left her jewellery to her daughter-in-law. Sir Morton bought it over forty years ago and it was insured with us for forty-eight thousand pounds. Valuation for probate might be well over that sum. Sir Morton used to travel all over the world as his own salesman, and he was rather a flamboyant character, as you know. He liked his wife—a very handsome woman—to cut a dash with foreign bigwigs, maybe to show the solid financial standing of his company. She often flew his private plane when the party was small. I don't know if you remember it, but about six years ago she was slightly injured in a crash-landing: broke her hip. Since the accident she wasn't very mobile and never left the house.

"You may think some of this irrelevant, and it may be. That'll be for you to judge. But to get back to the jewellery. This is the list."

He handed us each a list with descriptions and individual valuations. It was a remarkably short list: just a small tiara, a necklace and two matching earrings.

"They must have been pretty fine stones," Hallows said.

"They were. Sir Morton wanted plenty of—" he smiled dryly—"shall we say, sparkle, for his money. Neither the tiara nor the necklace was graduated. The stones were as near matched as could be and around six carats, and all the settings were platinum. As you see, there were nine in the tiara and twelve in the necklace. Each stone that formed an earring was slightly larger. It's believed that Sir Morton acquired the stones abroad—maybe as part of some deal or other—and had them made up here. The firm of John Parwell handled it.

"The last time the jewellery was cleaned, and by John Parwell, was for the Queen's coronation, for which Sir Morton and Lady Crewe had seats, if that's how one puts it. And that brings us to the happening of last Saturday morning, which is the reason why I'm seeing you here." He hesitated for a moment and looked at his notes. "Perhaps I ought to point out something else first.

"I've said that Lady Crewe was something of an invalid for the last few years of her life, so she never had occasion to wear the jewellery. She gave certain smaller pieces, by the way, to the daughter-in-law after Sir Morton's death—rings, bracelets and that kind of thing, and insurance was adjusted. The pieces we're concerned with remained at Sir Morton's town bank in Old Street in the usual sealed envelope.

"Now Julia Crewe was thinking of disposing of the jewellery, and thought it ought to be re-examined and possibly cleaned, so she and her cousin, Alan Cofield, came to town last Saturday morning and collected the sealed bag from the bank and then went on to Saffron Row. They'd telephoned and were expected. I should add that Mrs. Crewe and her cousin were lunching in town and then going on to a matinée: at any rate, they arrived at Saffron Row at about a quarter to twelve. Mr. Daunt wasn't there. He was seeing a client—what's known as an old and valued client: lunching with him at the Café Royal, in fact. Not that his absence should have mattered. He has every confidence in his head assistant—a Henry Bendale, whom you'll see later—just as his father-in-law, the late John Parwell, had."

He paused for a moment and I wondered why he was giving that dry smile of his.

"I hope I'm not getting all this out of proportion. Please don't think that the fact that the firm had been told the Crewe jewellery was being brought along that morning, put the whole establishment in an uproar. As far as they were concerned, the Crewe jewellery was just an item. If you know firms like John Parwell you'll have some idea of the value of the stock they might be carrying."

"Anything up to a quarter of a million?" I suggested.

"There've been occasions when it's been more," Hill told me. "Still, to get on. Bendale took the sealed envelope from Mrs. Crewe. That was in Daunt's office. He opened the envelope in her presence and that of Mr. Cofield and took out the three cases. He admits that he opened only one case, just by way of formal check; then he put the cases in the envelope again and put the envelope in the small wall safe. He locked the safe—"

"Just a moment," Hallows said. "Am I right in suggesting there were two safes?"

"That's right. A large modern safe which was used principally for antique silver or gold plate. That can be very bulky stuff and at the time that safe was pretty full. The smaller, wall safe dates from heaven knows how far back. Late Victorian probably."

He gave his dry smile again. "These old-established firms, especially where the principals live to a great age, hate the thought of any change. Twenty years ago the second safe was a Victorian monstrosity of an affair and John Parwell had it replaced by the present one because even it wasn't large enough. I gather he was what's known as a tight-wad. He talked as if the cost of that new safe was ruination and bankruptcy. Later on he got quite proud of it. Used to make excuses to show it to clients. But to get back to Saturday morning.

"Bendale put the envelope in the small safe, locked the safe and then gave Mrs. Crewe a formal receipt—"

"Sorry to interrupt again," I said, "but how many keys were there to that safe?"

"Two only." Hill told me. "Bendale had one and Daunt the other. As an extra precaution against loss, a spare key was kept at the firm's bank in Old Bond Street. At any rate, the safe, as I said, was locked. A very few minutes later the premises were locked up too. Everything closed down on Saturdays at twelve o'clock. On the Monday—yesterday—morning, Daunt arrived at about nine-thirty. Bendale told him the Crewe jewellery had arrived for cleaning, so the two men went into Daunt's office and Daunt took the envelope out of the safe. He took out the cases and opened one of them. Then he quickly opened the other two. Believe it or not, the diamonds weren't diamonds at all. They were just high-class paste!"

"Good lord!"

"It's been a surprise."

I'd been ahead of Hill for some time, and what I'd told myself was that when the cases were open, they'd be empty.

"No possibility of Bendale making a mistake?" Hallows wanted to know. "I refer to Saturday morning when he opened one of the cases and looked at the contents."

"Oh, no." Hill said. "A man like Bendale doesn't mistake paste for the real thing. He's been in the trade for over forty years. I don't want to teach you people your business, but I really do suggest you assume that what Bendale put into the safe on Saturday morning was the real thing."

"What about the cases themselves?" I said. "Were they the same ones?"

"Absolutely. The original ones supplied when the firm completed the making up of the diamonds forty years or so ago. There's no record, mind you, but the cases are of the type as then supplied and they carry the firm's name."

Hallows was referring to his notes. He asked if something could be made quite clear.

"John Parwell cleaned the jewellery just before the Coronation—say ten years ago. What happened then? Was it returned to the bank? And by whom?"

Hill consulted his own notes. "It was returned within a few days, and by Sir Morton himself. The bank records show it. The next time it was removed from the bank was in 1960, when Mrs. Julia Crewe was in England for her father-in-law's funeral. There was naturally some talk about the jewellery, and Mrs. Crewe expressed a wish to see it again, so it was fetched from the bank. The records show that it was handed to Mr. Alan Cofield and brought back by him two days later, and it remained in the bank till Saturday morning. You will recall that Lady Crewe was a semi-invalid and Mr. Cofield, her nephew, was the natural person to carry out her wishes. Does that cover everything?"

"I think so."

Hill gave him a quizzical sort of look. "Then what are you frowning about?"

Hallows smiled. "Was I? I think I was wondering something else. The jewellery that was substituted for the real thing, for instance. It must have been made at some time, and almost certainly by Sir Morton's instructions. And therefore, since they made the originals, by the firm of John Parwell. Is there a record of it?"

"I'm glad you asked that," Hill told him. "There *is* no record. You remember the installation of the new safe? Well, another reason for it was that there'd been a serious fire. Among other things destroyed were the ledgers. In other words, there're no records of the firm's transactions earlier than about twenty years ago. Mr. Daunt rang me last night to say there's no record of his firm having made any replicas."

I was about to speak but Hill interrupted me. "I should have added something. John Parwell didn't actually make the originals in their own workshop. They'd have drawn designs and consulted with the client and then the actual work would have been fanned out. The same with any replicas, except that it'd be a straightforward job."

"I was thinking of elderly employees of the firm," I said. "Surely there must be someone who remembers the commission for the replicas?"

"Unfortunately, no. Edgar Strome, who was senior assistant and entirely in old John Parwell's confidence, died two years ago. Bendale took his place and, until recently, he never was in what you might call the inner councils. Strome was still in full harness when he died. I believe he was getting on for eighty."

He looked at his watch. It was ten minutes to eleven. "Any ideas yet of possible lines of enquiry?"

"Everything depends on Bendale," I said. "If he was dead sure he put genuine diamonds into that safe on Saturday morning, then we have to find out who effected the substitution—and how—between then and the Monday morning."

"What about employees?" Hallows said. "Someone obviously had a key to open that safe."

"You mean by getting temporary possession and taking an impression?"

"Something like that."

"I should say it's out of the question. There's only one other inside employee, a salesman who's immediately under Bendale. But let me make something perfectly clear. The firm handles only valuable stuff. It isn't a question of small profits and quick returns. Customers who come in for the first time usually enquire about something of real value. If they don't, then they're very politely ushered out. And perhaps given the name of some other firm."

"What about packers for home delivery or export?"

"There's a small warehouse two doors on, at No. 7. A middle-aged man who's handled that for a good many years is still in charge."

The buzzer went and Hill picked up the receiver.

"Right," he said. "Stall them in the waiting room if you can so that they can all come up together."

"Daunt and Bendale are here," he told us. "I hope the others will be here in a minute or two."

We didn't have to wait even that long. The buzzer went again almost at once. Hill gave instructions for everyone to be shown up.

I rose at once to give my long legs a bit of a stretch. I suffer from a flippant mind at times and the remark wasn't all that apt, and certainly not necessary.

"Where the carcase is, the eagles will be gathered together."

"Perhaps you're right," Hill told me dryly. "Except that there doesn't seem to be any carcase."

3

IN CONFERENCE

"THE Mother of the Gracchi," I said to myself as soon as I clapped eyes on Julia Crewe. "Or Volumnia, straight from *Coriolanus*."

She was very tall for a woman and thin almost to gauntness, but superbly erect and perfectly poised. There was something regal too about the smile and the slight inclination of the head when Hill introduced me. I knew she was well over fifty and she looked her age, and yet one would be queerly wrong to think of her in association with age, and maybe because she had such an absolute, ageless assurance and, in that room, a kind of domination. I was crossing a year or two ago to New York in the *Queen Mary* and among our fellow passengers—tourist class—were quite a number of middle-aged or elderly American widows, probably returning from some conference or other in Europe. They too, had struck me as amazingly self-assured and supremely competent. I made the quip—not too well received by Bernice, my wife—that, without turning a hair, they'd be ready at any moment to grab a rifle and start fighting off the Indians. Julia Crewe was like that. Whomever else the Mau Mau had scared in Kenya, she must have been one whom they had never turned for a single moment from the normal routine.

Alan Cofield, I knew, was forty-six, but whether you took him for older or younger depended a bit on the light. He was quite an attractive looking man, even if his elbows in their time had done a considerable deal of lifting. He had what's often called an air force moustache. To some it gives a somewhat amusing air of ferocity, but on him it looked peculiarly apt. It gave him a kind of aristocratically raffish look: a sort of do-or-die plus hail-fellow-well-met, provided you were the right kind of fellow. An athletic type too: just about six feet and a good pair of shoulders. Where the ladies were concerned he was still probably quite a lad.

Stephen Daunt was pretty big too, but with more than a suspicion of a paunch. There was a slight touch of Harold Macmillan about him: the greying, somewhat unkempt moustache, for instance, and the set of the hair on his head, and the look which was often more of a stare. I'd have guessed his age as the fifty-four which it was. His voice I didn't like. It was too abrupt, and there was quite a touch of the dictatorial in his manner. He wouldn't have been badly cast as Mr. Barrett of Wimpole Street. I should add that he looked quite at ease. Considering the circumstances in which we were met, that was quite a feat.

I liked the look of Henry Bendale, even if he was far from being at ease and was making too much effort to avoid showing it. Maybe that was what made me immediately sympathetic. He was just above medium height and utterly bald except for two greying tufts around his close-set ears. In his way he had an air of some distinction: clean-shaven and with features that I'd call Graeco-Roman. His voice was extremely pleasant and to me his whole manner carried conviction. I should say that those were my first impressions of the new arrivals. Some, I now know, were hasty and even biased. I admit they had to be hasty but I shouldn't have allowed Cofield's moustache, for instance, to give me even a brief attack of intellectual arrogance or to try mentally to replace his conventionally sober suit with flannel trousers and a tweed jacket with leather-padded elbows.

The introductions didn't take more than a couple of minutes and then Hill got us all seated. He was at his desk and the rest of us formed a widish semi-circle with Hallows and myself strategically in the middle. To my immediate right was Julia Crewe, with Bendale on her right. Daunt sat next to Hallows. That put Cofield between Hallows and Hill.

"We all know why we're here," Hill began. "Mr. Travers and Mr. Hallows are directors of a long-established detective agency: one that United Assurance have employed with absolute confidence for quite a number of years. I take it we're all agreed that for the moment, at least, everything should remain, so to speak, in the family. We hope, in fact, that this business can be cleared up without going to the police. Agreed?"

There were general mumbles. Julia Crewe was the only one who actually spoke. She had quite a delightful voice. I'd expected it to be a bit strident, but it wasn't.

"The most sensible thing that could have been done. I've every confidence in the way Mr. Hill is handling everything."

Hill gave his dry smile. "Let's hope Mrs. Crewe's confidence is going to be justified. In any case we're all intelligent people and, if we do our best, I'm sure the whole thing can be speedily cleared up. There's one condition, however, I feel necessary to lay down. The Broad Street Detective Agency which is handling things on my behalf, and I hope on yours too, can't work either in the absolute dark or without your co-operation. Mr. Travers, speaking for his agency, accepts the assignment on one condition, and I implicitly agree with him."

I hope I didn't bat an eyelid. It was the first I'd heard of it: a beautiful piece of extemporisation. I'd have been delighted to think of it myself.

"He is, in fact, to be given a free hand. He's to be free to go anywhere and to ask anybody any questions whatever that he thinks necessary. And he'll expect to receive answers. If that alarms you in any way, may I say that you can rely on his absolute discretion." The dry smile again. "You may have your own ideas about private detectives. If you have, all I can say is I think you'll find Mr. Travers, and his colleague, a refreshing experience. You'd like to comment, Mr. Travers?"

"Only to thank you for the way you've introduced us," I said. "And to assure everybody that we'll tread on as few toes as humanly possible. As a matter of general information I should add that Mr. Hallows and I have already been given by Mr. Hill a fairly comprehensive account of what's involved. I think Mr. Hallows is now ready to ask some exploratory questions."

We'd agreed on that beforehand. I wanted to see the reactions of those four people. There's often more in the way things are said than in the words themselves. There might be slips of the tongue or contradictions. An answer might have too glossy or too apt a glibness. An unnecessary reticence, perhaps: you never can tell. And faces can be very much an open book when you've had years of experience at my particular game. That's why, as Hallows got to his feet, I unobtrusively shuffled my chair somewhat back. I wanted everyone in plain view.

Bob Hallows speaks well. He has a logical and quickly ordered mind. "I'd like to begin with you, Mr. Bendale, and at a quarter to twelve last Saturday morning. You opened the sealed envelope in Mr. Daunt's office at Saffron Row. Was it strictly necessary to do that? Couldn't the envelope have been placed intact in the safe and a receipt given accordingly?"

"Well, yes."

"Then why did you open the envelope?"

Bendale was a bit flustered. "I really don't know. All sorts of reasons. Curiosity, partly, I think. I'd never actually seen the jewellery before, though I'd heard about it. Also there was an aversion to—well, what you might call a pig in a poke. The subconscious, you might call it. The jewellery was coming in for treatment and I must have preferred to give a receipt for it and not for just the envelope."

Bendale, I thought, had had his answers ready. Once he'd got under way, he'd gathered quite a head of steam.

"I understand," Hallows told him. "You slit open the envelope and took out the three cases. You have the cases with you, and the paste jewellery?"

He did. He produced them from his brief-case. Hallows asked him to place them on Hill's desk just as they'd been placed on the desk in Daunt's office.

"And now Mrs. Crewe and Mr. Cofield, will you be so good as to place yourselves exactly where you were on Saturday morning when Mr. Bendale opened one of the cases? . . . Thank you. And now open a case, Mr. Bendale, and try to act exactly as you did on Saturday."

Bendale opened a case, took a quick look at it and replaced it in the envelope.

"No, no," Hallows said. "Didn't you smile?"

Bendale blinked. "Smile?"

"Yes, smile. Even to your hardened eyes those were very handsome stones. You wanted to see them and you *were* seeing them."

"Of course he smiled," Julia said. "And he looked at us as if he wanted us to agree they were what you said. He actually moved the case slightly towards us."

"Just what I'm trying to establish," Hallows said. "Correct me if I'm wrong but the whole thing took only a very few seconds. Mr. Bendale opened the case, took a quick look, smiled, turned the case for a moment towards you and then put it back in the envelope. You then saw him place the envelope in the wall safe and lock it."

"That's just what happened."

"But both you and Mr. Cofield had a quick look at the contents of the case that Mr. Bendale opened. What was in that case?"

"The necklace."

"You'd seen it before?"

"Yes. I saw it and handled it a day or two after my father-in-law's funeral."

"And you're absolutely sure that the necklace you saw on Saturday morning was the same one?"

"Absolutely sure."

"And you, Mr. Cofield. Did you ever see the genuine necklace?"

"Why yes, old boy." He gave a little start as if realising the familiarity had been something of a *gaffe*. "Yes, I saw it. The same time that Julia saw it—Mrs. Crewe. I saw it again when it was taken to the bank."

"And you think the one you saw on Saturday morning was the same?"

"Absolutely." He took the replica out of its case. "Look at this. Nothing to it. No sparkle unless you put it in the light. It's dead. Not the same thing."

Hallows turned to Hill. "I'd like Mr. Travers to examine the replica while I'm asking Mr. Bendale one last question. It's this, Mr. Bendale. Would you be prepared to stake your reputation on the claim that the necklace you saw on Saturday morning was the real thing?"

"I'd have no hesitation," Bendale told him firmly. "It *was* the real thing."

Hallows smiled. "Thank you, all three of you. I'm sure we now all agree that something has been established beyond question. The jewellery that was locked in the safe just before noon on Saturday last was absolutely genuine. If one case was in order, we can take it that the other two were the same. Now we've got something on which to build. And now you, Mr. Daunt. The cases themselves. I don't ask you to swear to anything but is it your opinion that they're the original ones?"

"That's my opinion. I think I *would* be prepared to swear to it."

Hallows gave me a questioning look. I said I'd like to ask a quick question or two.

"Mr. Bendale, the originals were set in platinum?"

"The necklace definitely was."

"All the jewellery was."

That was Julia Crewe. Hill added his quota. The jewellery was so described in the policy.

"And the metal used in the replicas, Mr. Daunt?"

"An alloy resembling platinum. Probably aluminium and mercury. Something like that. But what's the point of the question?"

"Well, you have the necessary contacts. You might be able to trace a firm that made such alloys. That might ultimately give us a complete history of the replicas. You'll agree that they're very high-class work?"

"Yes. For what they are," he told me grudgingly.

"And whoever made them must have had the originals in his possession?"

"Certainly."

"And since your firm was the only one to whom the originals were ever entrusted, isn't it reasonable to assume that Sir Morton Crewe, for reasons of his own, decided to have the replicas made, and by your firm?"

"Don't keep saying *my* firm," he told me testily. "There're no records of that sort. I agree it's reasonable but it must have taken place over twenty years ago. Probably much earlier."

"There's never been any family tradition of replicas, Mrs. Crewe? You were never aware there'd been any?"

"Never. My mother-in-law never mentioned such a thing."

"And you, Mr. Cofield?"

"Never heard of them."

"Thank you," I said, and put the three cases back on Hill's desk. Hallows prepared to carry on.

"This is the apparently simple problem," he said. "This is what we have to start on, that the replicas, almost certainly in their own cases, were in the possession of a certain somebody, and that between noon on Saturday and nine-thirty yesterday that somebody managed to unlock the wall safe, take the genuine jewellery and substitute the replicas. Did you enter your office during that period, Mr. Daunt?"

"I certainly didn't."

"Have you alibis that would stand up in a court of law?"

Daunt stared. His face slowly reddened. "Just what are you trying to get at?"

"The truth," Hallows said.

"Then I object to your methods."

Hill rapped sharply on his desk. His face had reddened too. "That will do, Mr. Daunt. You know our agreement. If you wish to break it, that's all right with me. We'll let the law take over."

Daunt made a last exasperated gesture. "You know we can't do that."

"Then the alibis," Hallows reminded him.

"I was at the Café Royal till half-past three, then I went home to my flat. My late uncle's flat: Valery Place, South Kensington. I'd had a tough day one way and another and I didn't leave the flat till the Monday morning. My wife can vouch for it."

"And you, Mr. Bendale? Did you return to the office?"

"Oh, no. Most certainly not. My wife and my daughter can vouch for it."

"Well, that's established something else," Hallows told us. "You two people were the only ones who had keys both to the premises and the wall safe?"

They were.

"Nobody else whom you can think of could have had the two necessary keys?"

Nobody.

"But couldn't there have been a certain amount of confusion when you uncle died, Mr. Daunt? You took over and Mr. Bendale was promoted. Couldn't someone then have had possession of the keys sufficiently long to have taken impressions, shall we say, and have had his own keys made?"

"Absolutely ridiculous," Daunt told him. "There wasn't any confusion. I was here when my uncle died. The changeover was just routine."

"And both you and Mr. Bendale can swear that during the period Saturday to Monday, your own keys never left your possession?"

Both could.

"Then that's about all," Hallows said. "Except a question for you, Mrs. Crewe. Whose idea was it to have the jewellery refurbished?"

She looked surprised. She gave a quick glance across at Cofield.

"It might have been mine. Or Alan's. Or both of us. I can't really say. I think it was one of those spontaneous sort of things."

"Was your husband consulted?"

"Not consulted. He was told, of course. He's somewhat of an invalid, you know."

"Thank you, Mrs. Crewe. I think that's about all, except for one last question to you, Mr. Daunt. Who knew that the Crewe jewellery was coming in on Saturday morning?"

"I took the telephone message," he said, "and I informed Mr. Bendale. I knew I had an engagement."

"Nobody else knew?"

"Why should they? There was no one else concerned." He cleared his throat. "If that's your last question, I'd like to say something. I think you people sometimes talk about inside jobs, and I'd like to point out that if someone did get possession of the necessary key's he could have chosen a far better opportunity to make a haul."

"I get your point," I told him. Not that I agreed. Those diamonds, taken from their settings, were about as good a haul as even the most ambitious could hope to make. But I didn't want to argue. The meeting was breaking up. I asked Daunt if it would be convenient for Hallows and myself to see him at his office in the early afternoon. Mrs. Crewe said she'd be delighted to see us in the morning, and then Hill was showing the callers out.

What had I learned about them? It was hard to say. Julia Crewe was very definitely in no way implicated. Cofield I wasn't so sure of, though how he could have worked the act was altogether beyond me. Astute was how I thought of him, and that's a long way from what had had to be organising genius. Bendale I thought absolutely in the clear: as for Daunt, surely there wasn't any reason why he should smirch his own good name.

Hill came back. He invited us to lunch and we accepted. But we didn't go down at once. Naturally he was anxious to know if we had any ideas, especially those not already openly expressed. I frankly didn't know.

"On the face of it and after what we've heard this morning it ought to be the simplest case we've ever had. The object wasn't to take just anything. It was the Crewe jewellery that was the target. And only those four people knew it was being brought along. And only two of them could have made the substitution. But they didn't. And neither of them knew anything about the existence of the replicas."

"I agree," Hallows said. "But what I think may be a very good clue is something we all knew before those people arrived—the fact that the jewellery was handed in on Saturday morning."

"Of course," Hill said. "Of course!"

"You're dead right," I told Hallows. "Mrs. Crewe and Cofield didn't get to Saffron Row till almost closing time. And on a Saturday. Both saw where the jewellery was placed. And they guessed it'd remain there undisturbed till yesterday morning. There were nearly two whole days in which to effect the substitution."

"Not collusion, surely," Hill said. "I can't imagine Mrs. Crewe being a party to anything of the kind. Cofield perhaps—yes. He looked a very—well, an unstable type."

"Even so, he still had to be in possession of various vital things," I said. "Two keys and the replicas. The replicas possibly, but if anyone can tell me how he could have got possession of the key to the premises and the key to the safe, I'd give him some very warm thanks."

"The golden handshake, if I was concerned," Hill said, and then we went down to lunch. During the meal we did an Omar—talked and talked and came out by the same door wherein we went. I did happen to think of just one thing. As I told Hill, Sir Morton and his wife wouldn't have been alone on those trips abroad. They must often have been accompanied by at least a small group of experts, including Sir Morton's own confidential secretary. If anyone could throw light on the history of the replicas, he'd be the man.

"Since Crewe Aircraft was taken over by United British only three years ago," I said, "it's possible Sir Morton's confidential secretary went there too."

Hill said he'd give them a ring. That was just before the meal ended. If I dropped in or rang later that afternoon, he ought to have some news. I was quite pleased about that idea. The more we knew about those replicas, the better.

We arrived at Saffron Row just after two o'clock. No. 5 was a two-storeyed building. Above the door, exactly between the twin windows, was what looked like the virtually original sign—

JOHN PARWELL
SILVERSMITHS AND JEWELLERS
(Founded 1805)

It had consistently been repainted, of course, just as the front of the building itself must have been remodelled, maybe in mid-Victorian times. Each window was fairly heavily grilled, and each displayed various pieces of silver. There was no jewellery. The upper half of the entrance door was glazed.

Inside was one quite large room. Along the left half of it was a counter, covered with green baize, and behind were shelves on which was displayed more silver. The rest of the room was shelved too, and there were a couple of display cabinets. They looked like Chippendale, as did a couple of chairs. About everything was an air of decorum. The dark-suited, middle-aged man who'd been behind the counter examining a set of spoons, merely looked mildly up as we entered. A bell had rung as we'd come in, and now Bendale suddenly appeared from a door in the background.

"It's all right, Clark," he said. "I'll see to these gentlemen."

The door turned out to be a short passage. At the end of it was Daunt's office: a large and really beautifully furnished room. The knee-hole desk was definitely Chippendale, as were a couple of wing grandfather chairs. Half a dozen prints, framed in bird's-eye maple, looked just a bit incongruous. The wall-to-wall carpeting was reasonably new but good. A serpentine-fronted cabinet occupied most of the left hand side of the room, and displayed in it was the first jewellery I'd seen. There was no disfigurement of filing cabinets—records, we were told, were kept on the upper floor. A late eighteenth-century Chinese lacquer screen reached across and back at the far right. Behind it was the safe.

We shook hands ceremoniously with Daunt. The room looked just the milieu for him. I congratulated him on it.

"As a matter of fact, my office in Edinburgh was even better," he told us. "The original sixteenth-century panelling. Quite a show place."

"You're still carrying on there?"

"Most certainly. We have a very good man there now—a Scot himself. Various things still to settle, of course. I may have to go up there for a week in a few days' time."

"You've been here long?"

"About ten years. Before that I was with British Silversmiths for over twenty years. But sit down, gentlemen. May I offer you a drink? A brandy?"

"Thanks, no," I said. "We're only staying a few moments. I think this morning gave us most of the information we want."

He might hardly have been the same man. Much less pompous. That room, I thought again, was just his milieu.

"What we would like to see are the two safes."

"Allow me," Bendale said, and led the way to the screen. Daunt followed.

That three-fold screen was eight feet tall, but it moved easily back. The safe itself was indeed a massive affair: a miniature Gibraltar.

"No need to open it," I said, and made my look a quizzical one. "What are the contents worth?"

Daunt shrugged his shoulders. "What do you think, Bendale?"

Bendale shrugged his shoulders. "I don't know, Mr. Daunt. Those Paul Lamerie pieces cost at least ten thousand. Say seventy-five thousand?"

I had to smile.

"You must give me the combination some time. But seriously: why couldn't the jewellery have been put in here?"

"Purely as a security precaution, I'm the only one who knows the combination," Daunt said.

"And in an emergency?"

"In a minor emergency, a customer would have to wait. Anything else—if I were suddenly taken ill, for example—Bendale here would be given the combination. The situation hasn't arisen yet."

"Good. And now the small safe?"

It was behind a Baxter print—the well-known *Bridesmaid*—in the space between the long cabinet and the wall. Daunt took a ring of keys from his trouser pocket, selected one and opened it. It looked about eighteen inches square and went back about nine inches. It had two shelves. They were virtually empty except for a half-dozen jewel cases on the upper shelf.

"Which shelf did you put the Crewe jewellery on, Mr. Bendale?"

"On the lower shelf. Just here."

"And that's where you found the cases, Mr. Daunt?"

"That's right. Just on the side there."

"Would you mind locking it again so that Mr. Hallows can have a look?"

Hallows produced his glass. He spent a couple of minutes examining that lock.

"Nothing at all," he told me. "Without a shadow of doubt it was opened with a key."

So that was that. I asked what precautions were taken against burglary. Daunt apparently considered there was no need to take any. The wall behind his desk was twelve-inch brick and a similar one from other premises backed on to it. I needn't go into the other details, and the fact remained that there'd never been a burglary. Also there was ample insurance.

"That's about all, then," I said. "Just one other question. Did either of you happen to mention anything about the Crewe jewellery at home during, say, the Saturday?" I smiled. "Wives do gossip, you know."

Both kept business strictly to the office. So that was all. We said goodbye to Bendale and Daunt himself showed us out. As we walked towards Old Bond Street and a bus, we naturally began comparing notes. Hallows was as sure as could be that neither Daunt nor Bendale had been criminally concerned. Mind you, the Daunt I'd just seen had been from the moment I'd entered his office a different person from the man who'd left the office of John Hill. I'd allowed myself to have wrong ideas about him. He wasn't a climber who'd ingratiated himself with a probably dictatorial patriarch of an uncle.

Hill had corrected me gently when I'd said something of the sort during lunch. Hill has his own sources of information besides the Broad Street Detective Agency and he'd done quite a lot of ferreting during the previous twenty-four hours. Caroline Daunt, he told us was John Parwell's stepdaughter. Daunt hadn't been merely the manager in charge of the Edinburgh branch: he was also Parwell's nephew and regarded as the heir. The reason why he hadn't joined his uncle's firm earlier was twofold. While the Edinburgh man—a very old associate—was still alive, there was no suitable niche for him. And Daunt was happy to be gaining experience in the responsible job he was holding down up to ten years ago.

But there was still something about Daunt that I vaguely disliked. Admittedly he hadn't shown himself to the best advantage during the morning, but that wasn't the reason for the curious aversion. I mentioned it to Hallows.

"Something physical?" he suggested. "You couldn't call him even a middle-aged Adonis."

That was it. Not so much a paunch—from which as yet I've been happily spared—as the sandy hair. I like red or auburn hair, especially in women, but, as I told Hallows, why there should be that curious dislike of sandy hair I hadn't any idea.

Hallows laughed. "Perhaps your mother was scared by a sandy-haired man."

"It's an idea," I said. "And there's his complexion. The sort of face that always perspires heavily. When I was a boy we used to call a man like that a *moist* kind of man."

Hallows smiled. "Well, provided his wife's satisfied, who else cares? She can't exactly be a beauty herself."

I didn't get it for a moment. "You mean because she's only twenty years younger than he is. Any port in a storm, so to speak."

I don't know why I kept thinking about the Daunts, but as the bus neared the Mansion House I suggested to Hallows that he might see John Hill personally and give him an account of our call on Stephen Daunt. And he might see if he could unearth anything else about the personal life of the Daunts. And he'd be hoping, of course, to get the whereabouts of the late Sir Morton Crewe's confidential secretary.

I went on to nearby Broad Street. I'd left my IN tray almost full, and I'd have to get really down to things if it was to be cleared before I picked up Hallows in the morning.

4
PENTLOW HOUSE

HALLOWS rang me just before five o'clock and gave me some news. Sir Morton's late confidential secretary was a man named Bertram Caplin. He'd been well on the way to seventy when he'd left Sir Morton's employ, and that was about four years ago when his chief was already ill. He apparently had not sought re-employment. Hill had thought that enquiries at Pentlow House might produce something.

"Anything more about the Daunts?" I asked him.

"I'm making some private enquiries," he told me: "that's what's kept me so long. I'm ringing from Fleet Street and I might be some time yet. I'll be seeing you in the morning in any case."

I picked him up at nine-thirty in the morning as arranged. It was a cold but clear November morning. There had been a certain amount of ground frost but the roads were perfectly safe. I didn't want to get entangled in the Watford or A40 traffic so drove by way of Harrow and Rickmansworth and then swung north towards Chesham. A large-scale map had shown me the little branch road to Newhurst, so there weren't any problems. I could do quite a lot of word-painting about at least the latter part of that drive if I were pushed. All I'll say is that the sun was out, the changing colours of the trees, especially the beeches, set that lovely countryside afire, and across the green stretches of meadow-land the gossamers twinkled as the light caught them. Once we were on that side road we drove quite slowly. Broad Street was suddenly an awful long way away.

Hallows had long since given me the briefest outline of what he'd unearthed about the Daunts. When he'd left me the previous afternoon, he'd rung John Hill instead of seeing him, and then had taken a bus back to the Strand and Somerset House. Then he'd walked on to Fleet Street and consulted certain newspaper files—picture papers mostly. What he had finally come up with was this.

He'd begun with the marriage of Stephen Daunt in 1961. His wife had been described as Caroline Gannon, aged thirty-three. From there he'd checked up on the marriage of John Parwell, which was in 1934. He had married an Elizabeth Carter, and that had made something radically wrong. Since Caroline was her daughter, Daunt should have married a Caroline Carter. The solution seemed to be that Caroline had been previously married, and that since she had been described as a single woman, she had actually been divorced. Her husband had been named Gannon.

That was what had taken Hallows on to Fleet Street. He has friends there and plenty of sources of information, and by the time he'd taken the Tube for home—which wasn't till after eight o'clock—he'd had virtually the whole story. As a driver himself he had more sense than to talk very much in traffic, and it wasn't till we were clear of Rickmansworth that we did any real talking, and only when we were nicely along that country lane that I pulled the car up and had a look at the press cuttings.

We weren't in any great hurry. I had rung Julia Crewe to say we'd arrive at about eleven, but we'd made good time and were only five miles from Newhurst. Ten minutes later I had changed my ideas about the Daunts.

Caroline Carter had hoped to become a ballet dancer. She worked at it till she was eighteen and then decided perhaps that it wasn't after all her métier. At any rate, she switched to modelling. She'd done fairly well at it even if she hadn't exactly set the glossy magazines on fire. Then in 1956 she'd married Patrick Gannon, whom you may remember as the British welter-weight champion. Since news had been scarce at the time, some papers had splashed that marriage across the front pages. Gannon also was at the time very much in the news, since he was lined up for a fight for the world title. Apparently, too, he was a bit of a playboy.

Radiant is the standard word applied to brides. Radiance didn't interest me so much as the startling fact that this bride was a remarkably handsome woman. I say startling, because such a thing had never entered my mind. And she'd still be so. Thirty-five is about the full flowering age.

Gannon's world fight hadn't matured but he went on to win the European championship. Meanwhile Caroline continued with her modelling. Two years later the marriage broke up and Caroline secured a divorce. A year later Gannon was killed in an accident that smashed his Bentley. Three years is a longish while to be a factor in a rebound marriage, but for her own reasons Caroline Gannon had married Stephen Daunt. Anyone more unlike Gannon could hardly be imagined.

"Any chance of getting any kind of story behind it?" I asked Hallows.

"As a matter of fact," he said, "I rang John Hill as soon as I'd got wind of the Gannon divorce. He's making enquiries. I think she saw certain advantages. Also, Parwell may have been behind the whole thing. After all, it was a marriage of a nephew and a step-daughter. Sort of kept everything nicely together."

That was true enough. After it, old John Parwell could sing his *nunc dimittis*. But we left things there. Time was running on and it doesn't do a firm any harm to have punctual directors.

Pentlow House lay just beyond the little village. It had its own short private road which continued on towards the church whose tower could be seen just above the trees a couple of hundred yards away. It was a medium-sized early Georgian house—a dozen or fifteen rooms all told perhaps—in a perfectly lovely setting. From the slight rise on which it stood one saw through the gaps of woodland a good five miles across the countryside. Its gardens didn't look large but there was quite a range of outbuildings away to the right.

An elderly butler admitted us and showed us into what he called the small drawing-room. It was a lovely, airy room with half-panelling and a superb fireplace. I ran my collector's eye round it and wished I could sneak up by night with a pantechnicon. Then Julia Crewe was coming in. We shook hands and she was sure we'd like coffee.

"What a beautiful place you have here," I said, "and what a delightful room. Did your father-in-law furnish it himself?"

"Oh, yes," she said. "He had the very best advice, of course. And my mother-in-law was very much of a connoisseur." She gave her little warble of a laugh. "Or should one say connoisseuse?"

We bandied the argument about for a minute and then the butler—Robert—came in with coffee. It looked to me like a mid-Georgian set *en suite*. The cups were definitely Coalport.

"My idea of final paradise," I said. "A lovely room, a lovely fire, a gorgeous view. And charming company."

She laughed. "Not exactly my ingredients. But it's nothing now to what it was in my father-in-law's time. Servants everywhere then, both indoors and out. My mother-in-law made do with a butler and housekeeper and a couple of daily women from the village."

"All the same, I just can't understand why you're selling it," Hallows said. "If it were mine, it'd break my heart. You *are* selling it?"

"Indeed, yes," she said. "Two recent death duties have almost impoverished things. You may smile at that but there just won't be the money there was. Also our real home is Kenya.

It's where all our friends are. We've lived there in the good times and now we can't desert it in its bad. And what money there is will enable us to do quite a lot to our farm."

She broke off to look quickly round. "Ah, here's my husband! Come and join us, David."

We got to our feet.

"Please don't move," she told us quietly. "He's rather impatient of help."

He was walking very slowly with the help of a stout stick: a tall man who must once have been loose-limbed and perhaps a bit ungainly, and who now had little more than a cautious, slow and even painful mobility. But there was a distinction about his face: the high forehead, the prominent cheekbones and the dark, expressive eyes. There was much about him of a clean-shaven Abe Lincoln: that was what I thought as he neared me.

He halted while his wife made the introductions, then let himself sink gradually into an easy chair to the right of us by the fire. He let out a little breath of relief.

"You men chat by yourselves," his wife told him. "If you want me, darling, Robert can find me."

She began putting empty coffee cups on the tray and smilingly refused my help with the tray itself, but I did manage to open the door.

We settled ourselves again.

"And you two fellows are trying to clear up this unfortunate business of the jewellery," Crewe said. His voice was slightly asthmatic. "Sorry I can't offer you anything to smoke, by the way. When I was a young man at Oxford I smoked far too much. A pipe. It was the fashion then, you know. But please smoke if you wish. I assure you it won't disturb me."

I lighted my pipe. Hallows rarely smokes.

"My wife gave me quite a good description of you." He had a most attractive smile. It gave his face a peculiar warmth. "She has quite a gift for description."

"She's a remarkable woman, Mr. Crewe. Please don't regard that as an impertinence."

"Of course not," he told me. "She *is* a remarkable woman. During my spells of bad health she's managed our affairs wonderfully. Better generally than I should have handled them myself. But about this extraordinary business of the jewellery: to me it's something utterly incomprehensible."

"They say the age of miracles is over, sir," Hallows told him. "When we get to the bottom of it we'll find, as we've done before, that it's comprehensible enough. At least, we hope so."

"Yes," he said. He leaned slightly forward. "I take it we're talking in confidence?"

"Most certainly," I told him. "Talk as freely as you like, sir. Nothing will ever be repeated."

"Thank you," he said quietly, and leaned back in the chair again. "Investigation is not my concern, and, even if it were, I'm too hampered by this arthritis of mine. All I know about this business is at second-hand. I've never seen those two jewellers, for example. My wife has given her impressions of them, but what do you think yourselves?"

I told him quite frankly that in our judgment both were men of absolute probity. Compared with the gross business handled over the last few years, the missing jewellery was quite a small item. If Daunt, for instance, had wished to perpetrate any kind of fraud, he could have done so long ago, much more safely and more to his own advantage.

"Of course. But you think you're making some progress?"

I smiled wryly. "Ask us that question in a week's time and we may have an answer. After all, twenty-four hours ago we didn't know even the main facts of the case. But there *is* something in which you may be able to help us: the question, for instance, of whose suggestion it first was that the jewellery should be cleaned. Mrs. Crewe seemed to suggest it was something spontaneous: suggested by her and Mr. Cofield at the same time. Did you yourself hear or take part in the discussion?"

"No," he said. "It's my wife's jewellery and there wasn't any reason for me to be consulted. She did tell me she thought of having it overhauled by the jewellers. I also knew about the arrangements for taking it to town on Saturday morning."

He was going on. But he didn't. He hesitated for a moment. "I hate to seem to doubt your word, but I would like to be reassured on this matter of confidence."

"All I can say, sir, is this," I said. "Our goodwill over quite a number of years has been built on confidence. Our good name is our best asset."

"Forgive me if I appeared to question it, but I was about to mention the name of a distant relative—Mr. Cofield. I tell you frankly now that I don't like the man. I trust I don't show it. I think he's a sycophant. Perhaps sponger would be a better word. I've seen practically nothing of him: I had to form a judgment before coming here, from my mother's letters, especially since my father's death. She was always referring to him as helpful. Indispensable—that sort of thing. Always spoke of him as 'dear Alan'. I'm almost sure she gave him considerable sums of money from time to time. I've been going through her private accounts and the sums can't be accounted for: sums drawn in cash and not paid by cheque."

"And your father's opinion of him?"

"I think he treated him as a joke. An amiable joke. I've thought that that business of leaving him the Hollindale house was a kind of joke too: an abstruse one, perhaps, but a way of telling him the only thing he'd ever been good for was golf. He made him an allowance of a thousand a year, and left him five thousand. My mother continued the allowance and she also left him five thousand. He can't receive it, of course, till after probate."

"And meanwhile, he's hard-up?"

"Well, my guess is that he spent my father's legacy long ago. Probably clearing up debts. But even today he ought to be able to live on a net thousand a year. The gift of the house also included the keep, so to speak, of the two servants."

I thanked him for his confidences and said we'd keep the gentleman in mind. Then I put my other question. Did he by any chance know the present whereabouts of his late father's confidential secretary—a Mr. Bertram Caplin?

He stared, then actually laughed. "My dear fellow! Of course I do. Soon after we arrived he called to offer his condolences. He had dinner with us only last week."

"That's splendid!" I said. "It's rather urgent we should see him. Apparently he's the only one who might be able to tell us something about the replicas. The ones that were substituted for the jewellery."

"You can see him whenever you like. He's quite near here. A charming old cottage, my wife says. Little Dormers, Watfield. About five miles from here. All this area had lifelong associations for him, so he retired here. A delightful character. My father thought an enormous deal of him."

"You can arrange for us to meet him?"

"Of course. But let's go along to the morning-room."

I remembered just in time not to help him get up from the depths of the chair, but he managed it. Leaning heavily on the stick he made his slow way to the door and across the entrance hall and then to the right. That morning room was larger than my own lounge: comfortably furnished and with the same fine view across the fields. A knee-hole writing desk stood between the two tall windows, and Crewe had evidently been working there. There was a superb Bokhara carpet that covered practically all the floor and there were plenty of books. Robert must have made the fire up; it was burning so briskly.

Crewe swivelled the chair and sat. He reached for the telephone. "I hope he'll be in. What time shall I suggest? After lunch? About half-past two?"

He must have seen the quick look on my face. "You'll be staying to lunch, of course?"

"No, sir. We really couldn't impose on you like that."

"Nonsense," he said. "Sheer nonsense. Besides, it's already arranged."

Two or three minutes later he was hanging up the receiver. "There you are. Bertram will be delighted to see you at half-past two. I'm sure you'll enjoy his company."

"Just one thing," I said. "To what extent can we take him into our confidence?"

He thought for a moment. "Naturally you'll have to tell him the bare facts of the case. Speaking personally, there's nothing I wouldn't trust him with."

I said that was good hearing, and then Julia Crewe ran us to earth. She showed us round the house and then we all had a sherry and after that came lunch: an honest-to-God English meal and a dry Bordeaux. It was the friendliness of it all, and the informality, that was so pleasing. The case was never mentioned and not because the butler was generally hovering around. His full name, by the way, was Robert Lockyer. He was sixty-five and had been with the family over forty years. The housekeeper, whom we didn't see, had been with them even longer. My guess was that both would be well provided for.

We left at about a quarter-past two. We drove past the church, rejoined the village road and turned left for Watfield. We pulled up at a straight stretch about a mile on. We agreed that so far it had been a red-letter day, taking the pleasurable side as distinct from the business. We'd been received as guests by charming people in a lovely home, and we'd both enjoyed every minute of it. But what had we learned?

The answer was virtually nothing, except that Alan Cofield might be worth a lot more attention. We spent a minute or two in taking another quick look at him. The only thing against him was that he needed the money. How on earth he could have obtained those two vital keys from two people with whom he'd had no previous contact whatever was something still altogether beyond us.

We moved on towards Watfield. Julia Crewe had given us precise instructions and we had no difficulty in finding the cottage. It was a half-timbered building with a thatched roof and set back some thirty yards from the lane. A crazy-paving path led through the garden which still had plenty of colour, and farther to the side a gravelled way led to a garage. I drew the car off the narrow lane on the grass verge and we got out. Bertram Caplin must have been looking out for us. He was coming out of his front door just as we opened his gate.

I had been told that at seventy he was as brisk a man as David Crewe had ever known, and, from the way he came towards us, I guessed it was true. He was just below medium height, sparely built and with a shock of unruly white hair that gave him from a distance the look of an amiable cockatoo. His weather-tanned face was wrinkling with smiles.

We introduced ourselves and he was telling us to come along to the house.

"Pretty much of a change from Pentlow House," he told us, and drew back to let us through. "Still, I do have a cat and that's more than they have there. Sit down and make yourselves comfortable. Do you mind if I smoke?"

It was a typical country living-room. A small dining-room would flank it, and upstairs there'd be two—maybe three— bedrooms and a bathroom, and there'd be a kitchen and maybe another small room downstairs at the back. He told us a village woman did for him in the mornings and came back in the early evening to prepare his meal. At the moment we had the house to ourselves.

"You like it here?" I said.

"Yes, and no," he said. "This is my country where I've spent most of my life. When Sir Morton died, something went out of it. Now Laura's gone too—well, that's another break with the past. And now the house is going to be sold." He shook his head. "Maybe I'll spend my last years abroad. Mexico, perhaps. I always did like Mexico."

I had the job of explaining that we were not friends of David and Julia Crewe, as he might be imagining. In fact, I told him precisely why we were there, not that it hadn't given us great pleasure to meet him. While I was talking, his eyes didn't leave my face.

"Incredible!" he said. "The jewellery was positively put in the safe around midday on Saturday, and by the Monday morning the replicas had been substituted. And yet no one had been there and no one had the necessary keys but the jewellers."

"Yes," I said. "That's roughly it."

"Incredible!" he said again. "Seems to me you ought to be looking for some sort of magician. A Houdini."

"Maybe. But about those replicas. You knew about them?"

"Heavens, yes." He smiled. "Sir Morton had them made only a year or so after the originals. He was very secretive about it. I remember he warned me sternly never to mention them. He was like that. One moment he'd be blasting your head off and the next he'd be clapping you on the shoulder and telling you what a good fellow you were."

"But why did he have the replicas made?"

He explained. In those early days when the company's lifeblood was regular sales, some pretty unstable countries had to be visited. There'd been quite an unpleasant incident in Venezuela when a revolution happened to crop up at an awkward time. That's why the replicas were made and why they'd been well made. They had to pass muster when a situation warranted it.

"And who knew of their existence besides you three?"

"I doubt if anyone did. If anyone among us was smart enough to spot the difference, he'd also be smart enough to keep his mouth shut. No one certainly ever mentioned them to me. Of course, there'd be the jeweller who made them. He'd know."

"Do you think the firm of John Parwell made them?"

"Can't say. The odds surely are that they did. If so, I'll bet the Old Man—pardon me, just force of habit. It's logical that they made them, and what I was going to say was that they'd have been sworn to secrecy, like me. Sir Morton would have thought it the very worst kind of publicity if anyone had known his wife was going around wearing fakes. He worshipped her. And he was a very vain man. And proud. He had a right to be."

"But a good man."

"The best," he said quietly. "The William Morris of the aircraft industry. I know. I played a small part in shaping things. And the finest employer any man could have."

"A good epitaph," I said. "And it does you credit. But about the replicas. What happened to them?"

"Don't know," he said bluntly. "Just after the war he gave up all the previous kind of foreign travel. I suppose there wasn't any need for it."

He frowned in thought. "No, I can't recall when I saw those replicas last. Might have been as much as twenty years ago. I haven't an earthly idea. I never even heard them referred to. After all, we were busy people. By comparison, things like replicas of jewellery were just a triviality. And personal to him and Lady Crewe." He smiled. "You might as well ask me when I last saw him wearing a certain colour tie."

I saw the point. "And there's nowhere and no one you can suggest for any enquiries?"

"Sorry, no. If Laura—Lady Crewe—had been alive, she'd have known. I'm surprised in a way she didn't mention anything to anybody. David's wife, for instance. But perhaps I'm wrong. She'd respect Sir Morton's wishes. And paste replicas wouldn't be of any value."

That virtually concluded the visit. He wanted to make early afternoon tea for us and seemed most disappointed when we had to refuse: but, as I told him, November nights were treacherous and we ought to get back to town before dark. I did give him a card and he said he'd put his few wits to work and ring us the moment he had any ideas.

He waved a goodbye from the gate. A charming person— the third we'd met that day. A tragedy, I thought, of which at only rare intervals—as on that day—one becomes aware. The tragedy, or the sadness rather, that the world is full of delightful people whom one will never meet.

Pardon that digression. Just a not-too-scintillating facet of Ludovic Travers: this time the philosopher-manqué.

5

STRANGE ENCOUNTER

WHEN I'd told Bertram Caplin we wanted to make town before dark, I hadn't been telling "nothing but the truth". We still might make it, but, if we didn't, it wouldn't matter. What we had decided even before we saw Caplin, was to do the further seven miles to Hollindale and run an eye over that place of Cofield's—"Southways". We'd probably have to go there at some time or other, so why not take advantage of being practically on the spot.

It was about four o'clock when we reached the village. I used to play quite a fair amount of golf myself some years ago. I'd played only once at Hollindale when I'd happened to be spending a weekend near by with friends, but I began to remember things: where to turn off for the golf course and how there was a private road opposite a farm, with the club-house a short way along.

Those who'd founded that course had been more farsighted than most: they'd protected it by acquiring quite a lot of land at the village end of it. It still remained farmland. Even the railway and Hollindale's new hotel were quite a distance away. Southways wasn't. Sir Morton had retained a nice little plot for himself. The cosy little house he'd had built there lay at the end of the continuation of the clubhouse road: it actually overlooked the eighteenth green.

I drove towards the club-house and left the car in the parking lot. "Southways" itself stood in a natural clearing among some superb trees. It was a smallish house built of red brick with a roof in darker red tiles: somewhat in a Georgian style with a semi-circular, covered porch. It'd be just large enough to hold, say a, foursome of guests for a week-end. Its own gravelled drive split just before the house itself with the right-hand turning away to a smaller brick building of two low storeys. The lower half was obviously a garage that would hold up to four cars, and above were probably the quarters of the married couple who looked after the house.

There wasn't a large garden, and what there was, was mostly lawn. A few fruit trees separated the lawn from a small kitchen garden and the whole was enclosed in a brick wall some eight feet high. As we were running an eye over it all, a man emerged from behind the garage. It wasn't a warm day but he was in shirt-sleeves and carrying a birch broom. He'd probably been sweeping up leaves. Now he caught sight of us straight away. He hesitated for a moment and then came across the lawn. It

was Hallows he spoke to. "Excuse me, sir, but were you looking for Mr. Cofield?"

"As a matter of fact we were," Hallows told him. "We didn't
knock because we had an idea he'd be out."

"We've been lunching with Mr. and Mrs. Crewe at Pentlow
House," I said—the prestige might do us a bit of good—"and
that's how we thought he'd be out. We just took a chance."

His face had lighted. He was a man of about sixty: spare,
but well muscled and with a tanned country face.

"And how was everybody, sir?"

"You know them?" I said.

"Mr. David and Miss Julia?" He smiled. "I was brought up
with Mr. David, sir, so to speak. I used to be second gardener
and my wife, she was head housemaid. We were there all
our lives. Right up to when the old master died, and then we
came here."

"You knew Mrs. Crewe was selling the house?"

"Yes, sir, and mighty sorry I was too. Miss Julia drove over
last week and told me herself. But about Mr. Alan, sir. You may
find him somewhere round the third green. He went out to do
a bit of practising. There's a match of some sort on tomorrow."

We met Alan Cofield coming towards the club-house from
the rough to the left of the eighteenth green. He was wearing an old suit of brown plus-fours with a dark red pullover,
and was carrying a couple of irons. I thought he looked taken
aback when he saw us. A quick, wary look had preceded the
hearty greeting.

"Just a friendly call," I said. "We've been at Pentlow House
most of the day and I thought I'd like to see Hollindale again."

"You've played here?"

"If you can call it that. Quite a time ago though. I was one of
the hit-or-miss brigade. If I hit 'em they used to go: if I didn't,
they didn't. Not like tigers—like yourself."

"Don't flatter me, old boy. I'm getting a bit long in the tooth. But what about a spot of tea? Only a few yards to the house."

I hesitated. "Well, just a quick cup. We'd like to get back to town by dusk. We did just look in, by the way. Your man told us we'd probably find you on the course. He looks a very able sort of chap."

"Froden? Oh, yes. A very handy fellow. Looks after the garden, services my car—that sort of thing. Mary—she's his wife—is a damn good cook."

"Lucky fellow," I told him. We'd taken a path as a short cut and were already nearing the front door. He showed us into what he called the lounge: a largish room furnished in a not-too-modern way: comfortable and with a pleasant tobacco-like smell. A tan setter that had been sleeping on a rug before the fire came slowly towards us, wagging its tail.

"Sally isn't too fit," he told us and rubbed the dog's ears. "Usually she goes out with me. An absolute corker at finding lost balls. Make yourselves comfortable. I'll see Mary."

A couple of minutes after he'd come back, Mary Froden was bringing in the tea—just a large pot of tea, some bread-and-butter and what looked like a home-made plum cake. She was a pleasant-looking, plump woman of about sixty. There was just a hint of dusk already in the air and a little mist. She switched on the light and drew the curtains before she left.

"A great life you must have here," I told Cofield.

"I don't know, old boy. I think I can say I've earned it. Life didn't use to be all golf, you know: not in the old days."

There were various things I didn't want to do. I didn't want to mention Bertram Caplin, just as I hadn't thought it expedient to let Caplin know we were going on to Hollindale. Also I didn't want to mention the jewellery, at least till the last moment. I tried to talk about golf and waited to see if it would be he who brought the subject up. But there wasn't a word about jewellery till a quarter of an hour later when we'd said we'd really have to be going. Then Hallows took over with a question on which we'd agreed during those few moments before tea when Cofield had been out of the room.

Cofield came with us to our car. The slight tension he had shown when we'd talked briefly about the jewellery had altogether disappeared. He was on the best of terms with himself again.

"Come down some time and have a day here," he told me. "You come and caddie for him, Hallows, old boy. It won't cost you a cent."

"Very good of you," I said, "but it wouldn't be golf, it'd be murder. Good of you, all the same."

That was just as I was moving the car on. He waved a hand, and when I looked in the mirror as we turned out of the parking lot, he was striding briskly towards the house.

We drove on towards the village, past the hotel, and pulled up at the telephone kiosk outside the post-office. It was empty and I rang Pentlow House. The butler answered, then put me through to David Crewe.

I told him what we'd learned from Bertram Caplin and how we'd gone on to Hollindale. I asked him to use his discretion with both Caplin and Cofield. It might be advisable to let them do the talking if the matter of the jewellery cropped up. That way he'd know just what Caplin, for example, knew.

"Now one very important thing," I said. "You remember how we attached considerable importance to finding out who it was that suggested taking the jewellery to be cleaned?"

"I remember. We discussed it briefly."

"Well, we deliberately suggested to Cofield—sort of as between man and man—that it was your wife who suggested it. He went through the motions of thinking the whole thing out again and then he told us—strictly between ourselves—that it *was* Mrs. Crewe who made the suggestion. He said he was sure of it, but he didn't want it mentioned."

"He was lying."

"We know that," I told him. "It may be some help and it may not, but we thought you ought to have that amount of confidential information."

"Thank you," he told me. "I'm very grateful to you."

I was glad he hadn't laboured the point. Cofield's specific statement, added to what we'd learned of him directly from Crewe, seemed pretty important. For the first time we had something of a suspect. Cofield was a slippery customer who'd do with a considerable deal of investigation. Not that we credited him with being a latter-day Houdini. Still, one never knew.

We didn't talk much about the case. Dusk was already falling, and long before we reached the suburbs the day for us had gone. I've done enough philosophising but we'd had in many ways a wonderful day. We'd even for a time gone back forty or more years into a world I'd known only too well, and now it had ineluctably gone. The traffic, the suburbs, and an ultimate Broad Street were incredible years and spaces apart.

The next moves had to be planned and we got down to work. Hallows would go on ferreting out everything possible about the Daunts. I'd write up the case so far and try to find new methods of approach. I worked on till just after six o'clock and called it a day.

At three o'clock the following afternoon I was at a loose end. I'd interspersed normal work with reviewing the Crewe case but new ideas just hadn't come. Hallows had rung at midday. He said he'd had a brief session with John Hill: had unearthed various snippets of information elsewhere and was hoping to find more. He'd see me at around five o'clock and maybe we could collate them. I said I'd be in.

I was, but only for another ten minutes. One of the things I'd been hunting for was an excuse to see Daunt in his own apartment, since that would have meant meeting his wife. I couldn't for the life of me think of an excuse which might seem perfectly natural but somehow I wanted to get out of an office where I'd been all day. Then it struck me that I might at least have a look at that apartment where Daunt now lived.

I got out at South Kensington Station and wondered just where Valery House might be. A chance postman told me. In the area behind the old Imperial Institute were two or three blocks of flats and Valery House was one of them. I hadn't been that way for some time but it looked fairly new: say about ten years old. It had the usual small carpark in front of the main entrance and a still smaller extension at the right-hand side. Good-class flats in that area are most expensive, and I wondered again why a tight-wad like old John Parwell had been prepared to spend, say, eight hundred a year which couldn't appear in his expense account.

I'd thought his apartment was No. 7 but a reference to my note-book showed it as 17. I went through the entrance doors and across the hall and past the small office where a girl was sitting at the desk, and on up a flight of stairs. It was all very sedate and my feet made never a sound on the thick carpet. I went round three sides of the oblong and moved on to more stairs. Flat 17 was on the floor above. I went up. I went along a corridor and turned. A woman in a fur coat came out of a door and moved towards the lift. I followed till I came to the door from which she'd emerged. It was No. 17.

I took the stairs again and approached the desk.

"I'm looking for Flat 17," I told the girl. "Mrs. Daunt."

"Mrs. Daunt has just gone out," she said. "If you hurry you might catch her."

I hurried but only as far as the door. Caroline Daunt was crossing the road. She walked a few yards to the right, to the bus stop. I waited till a bus drew up and then managed to spring across the road. I was in time to see her moving to the front. I went on top. The bus was going to Oxford Circus so I took a ticket accordingly. I could always pay extra and go on.

She got off at Oxford Circus, crossed with the traffic lights and went down Regent Street. I followed at a fair distance. I didn't expect anything more than a late afternoon's shopping but, if she did enter a store, I'd at least contrive to have a good look at her. So far I'd seen only her back. She carried herself well even if she seemed in something of a hurry.

We went past Liberty's and on to that recess that cuts back to a Fuller tea-shop. Suddenly she was veering left towards a man. He came a pace or two to meet her: a tall man wearing a snap-brimmed hat and one of those light-coloured, three-quarter length overcoats that seem to be fashionable. His hand went out and she shook it petulantly off. They stood there for quite a minute, still keeping their distances, then turned into the recess. She seemed reluctant. He made as if to take her arm again, and again she shook it angrily off.

I'd been a good fifty yards away so I quickened my pace. I was just in time to see them entering Fuller's, and I was on their heels as they made for a table at the far end of the smaller room which always seems a kind of annexe. I turned sharp right into the larger room. In a mirror I could see their table, and a lucky chance of a couple just leaving gave me a table quite near. My back was towards them and not all that distance away. I had them plainly in view. My reflection, I was pretty sure, wouldn't be visible. Not that I worried overmuch. I had as much right as Caroline Daunt to be in that shop.

I had them both in profile. I'd never have recognised her, at least from that distance, as the bride whose picture Hallows had shown me, but she was definitely a remarkably good-looking woman. The man was about her own age. His dark hair was swept back and the moustache he wore was neatly trimmed. It was he who seemed to be doing all the talking. She was indifferently, or even sulkily, listening.

My waitress arrived, and it was not till I'd settled down to the pot of tea and slice of cake that I could watch that couple again. I had to eat quickly and be prepared to abandon a second cup. At any moment, it seemed to me, the lady was likely to get up and leave. Then all at once, as the man turned a bit more full-faced—he was fumbling in his pockets for something—I had the idea that I'd seen him somewhere before. And just then the lady did get to her feet. I gulped down the last of my only cup and made urgent signals to the waitress. By the time I'd paid my bill at the desk the couple were just disappearing round the corner.

I hurried along in the same direction and, by a stroke of luck, a man baulked me at the corner: if not I might have barged full tilt into the couple. Just round the corner they were continuing their argument. I turned quickly back and neither of them seemed to notice me. I leaned against the wall as near as I could to the corner and began consulting my evening paper. I didn't hear anything at first. Then tempers seemed to be rising.

"You're going to be damn sorry about this, you know. Damn sorry."

"So will you be if you pester me any more."

"I'll do what I damn well please."

She must have been moving away.

"And that goes for your boy-friend, too."

A moment of two and he was going past me towards Oxford Circus, and again, as I had a good side-faced view of him, I was sure I'd seen him somewhere before. I looked down the street for a sight of Caroline Daunt. She must have slipped into some store or other: at least, she was no longer walking down Regent Street. When I turned, the man had disappeared too.

I told Hallows about that curious encounter. I'd jotted down the few words I'd heard so that I shouldn't forget them. They'd been at the corner, I said, only a few seconds. "And you really think you know the man?"

"I've met him or seen him somewhere," I said. "I never was more sure of anything. A man of about thirty-five, dark-haired and a neat dark moustache. About six feet. Also he seemed to have a slight American accent. American or Canadian."

He shook his head. "Conveys nothing to me. Mind if I have a look at what was said?"

He read what I'd jotted down. "Whoever he was, he seems to've been pestering her and she got fed-up with it. All the same, she did meet him, and by appointment. Do you think he had some kind of hold over her? The way he threatened her, for instance?"

"Could be," I said. "What seems just as important, though, is that bit about a boy-friend. I think he called it after her as she was moving away."

"Any point in putting a tail on her?"

I didn't think so. The man she'd met might contrive to thrust himself on her but I doubted if she'd see him again. Then I had an idea. It was just about half-past five. Daunt would probably be thinking of going home. It was just the right time to ring him.

I got him almost at once. The usual conventional words and I came to the point.

"I'd rather like to see you for a minute or two. Just a report on what we learned yesterday. Do you think I might drop in on you this evening? Any time that suits yourself. Before dinner, for instance?"

"Half-past six suit you? Or is that too early?"

We compromised on a quarter to seven. I said I shouldn't be keeping him more than a few minutes.

"I'll now have a good chance to see the lady at close quarters," I told Hallows. "And to form an idea of the manage. Did you unearth anything special yourself?"

He began with what I knew: that John Parwell had married fairly late in life: a widow with a small daughter. She died in 1959. He'd been living in Putney but the long journey to town was getting too much for him. He'd had quite a serious illness after his wife's death. It was about that time that Caroline had managed to extricate herself from her boxer.

"I gather she spent some time in Putney," he told me, "and I'd say it was she who got him to take a flat handy for his business. When they leased the flat, she joined him. I can't trace any more modelling so probably she was there just to look after Parwell generally. She might have had an eye on her expectations. Daunt, as the old man's nephew and right-hand man, was often there too and then, when the old man really went sick, she came back from Edinburgh, where she and her husband were living, and stayed at the flat till he died. That's why the Daunts are there now: maybe using that much of the lease still to run."

"I see. And was she often at Saffron Row itself?"

"Hardly ever, so Bendale told me. I took him to lunch, by the way, to get most of what I've been telling you. The only other thing I got was the name of Caroline Daunt's friend who gave evidence on her behalf at the divorce proceedings. She's a woman named Helen Vaile. She's an authoress: writes love romances. Present address—if you'd like to take it down—Windover, Ludwold, Nr. Berkhamsted. It may help and it may not."

That was about all. I had to smarten myself up a bit, and quickly, if I wasn't to be late. As a matter of fact I was a minute or two early when I pushed the bell of the Daunt flat. Daunt himself let me in. I'd forgotten that he had a moist hand.

It was a flat, I gathered, of five rooms: a quite large lounge, two bedrooms, bathroom and kitchen. Meals were available in a downstair restaurant. Servicing was provided by the management. The lounge itself was very comfortably furnished. The easy chairs and the large chesterfield had covers of handsome chintz that matched the curtains of the two tall windows in the far wall. The carpet was modern Chinese with a pink motif that matched the chintz. There was a reproduction Sheraton sideboard from which Daunt was producing drinks; a radio-gramophone, and a large television set on a metal stand. The electric fire was a large, silvered, imitation eighteenth-century basket.

He gave me the gin and French I'd suggested.

"Just a moment," he said, "and I'll call my wife. She's in the kitchen. We're just having a snack tonight. I don't think you've met her."

He opened a door just beyond the radiogram.

"Carry! Can you come a minute?"

Caroline's a charming name. I think I winced. *Carry* reminds me of poke-bonnets and mittens. At any rate we had only a minute to wait before she came in. If she'd been engaged in serious cooking, she'd made a quick and marvellous hand at transforming herself. Every hair and eyebrow seemed in place and there wasn't a wrinkle in the gown. And she was even better-looking than I'd thought. The smile couldn't have been more delightful.

"This is Mr. Travers, one of our latest clients," Daunt said. "My wife, Mr. Travers."

She and I took corners of the chesterfield. Daunt brought the gin and lime she'd asked for. We raised our glasses. I started the conversational ball rolling by indicating the radiogram and asking if they liked music. Daunt smiled a bit wryly.

"I'm afraid there's a conflict of opinion," he said. "I like classical music and Carry here, likes modern stuff. Still, we usually manage to compromise."

"Like my wife and myself," I said unblushingly. "Each plays what we like when the other one's out."

She laughed. "Now I call that real compromise. We'll have to try it, Stephen."

Daunt made no comment. I think he frowned slightly. A queerly assorted couple, those two, I was already thinking. And with conversation not too easy to make.

"You like it here, Mrs. Daunt?"

She did, and she told me why. Chiefly because it was so handy for everything. That brought us somehow to theatres. We'd just got to American musicals when Daunt got to his feet.

"Sorry to disturb you, my dear, but Mr. Travers is in rather a hurry. If you don't mind leaving us for a minute or two . . ."

She gave me a smile and got to her feet. I rose too, of course, but rather slowly and with a slight look of puzzlement.

"Do you know, Mrs. Daunt, I'm sure I've met you before." I gave a quick, remembering smile. "Of course. Weren't you in Regent Street this afternoon? About four o'clock. I'm sure I passed you."

For the merest second she'd been knocked clean off her perch. Another second and she was smiling incredulously. "Me? In Regent Street?"

"Well, a woman wearing a fur coat. Almost as charming as yourself. I actually turned to look at her."

She laughed. "I do have a fur coat, if that means anything, but it couldn't have been me. I haven't left the flat all day."

"Which just goes to show," I said. I turned to Daunt. "I'll have to cure myself of looking at pretty women."

He made a poor hand of a smile. I moved forward and opened the door for the lady. When I turned back, Daunt was across the room, pouring himself another whisky. He didn't ask me if I'd like another drink. Something must have been disturbing him. However, we got down to business and it didn't take long.

"So we did make the replicas," he said, "and it sounds as if it was a hush-hush kind of job. Certainly my uncle never breathed a word at any time to me."

"It was a long time ago," I pointed out. "He'd probably forgotten all about it himself. Did he leave any papers here when he died? Any personal records?"

"A few oddments," he said. "Nothing whatever that had any reference to the Crewe family. If I may say so, Sir Morton was only one client among what must have been many thousands."

"True enough," I said, and began getting to my feet. "I'm afraid that's all I have for you at the moment, but I thought you ought to know."

He helped me on with my overcoat and went with me to the door. He thanked me as we shook hands. I asked him to say goodnight for me to his charming wife.

I went a yard or two along the corridor, then turned back. I put my ear against the door.

"Carry! Carry!"

He was calling quite loudly to his wife. Then there was the sound of voices in the far corridor. Some people were coming and I went towards them—a couple of men and a girl. I turned back again when they'd disappeared round the corner in the direction of the lift, and clamped my ear against the door again. What was being said I couldn't hear but Daunt's voice was being angrily raised.

I was frowning to myself as I, too, made for the lift. I wondered if Daunt would ask a question at the desk and learn that his wife might after all have been the woman I'd seen in Regent Street.

It was after eight o'clock when I reached home. Bernice and I had a service meal and then watched television, and all the time I kept wondering where it was that I'd seen that man with whom Caroline Daunt had spent some minutes that afternoon. Perhaps, I thought, I'd never met him at all. In the flesh, that is. Maybe he was some television actor with whose features

I'd become slightly familiar. But it worried me till I went to bed. It was with me when I ultimately fell asleep.

Something was to happen that has happened to me many times before: in fact, it is always happening. I go to bed with a small, unsolved problem on my mind: the forgotten name of some person or other, perhaps, or the shaping of an anagram or some clue in a cross-word puzzle, and I wake in the morning with the answer there. That was how it was the next morning. I didn't think back: I didn't do anything.

I stirred in bed, reached for my horn-rims and sat up. Templett, I said to myself, just like that. Geoff Templett!

6

HITHER AND YON

I USUALLY contrive to get to the office round about nine, which means leaving the flat at half-past eight. That morning I left a quarter of an hour earlier. Tom Jordan's place is only about five minutes from Broad Street, but the talk I was likely to have with him might take some time.

I was so early that he wasn't yet in, but five minutes later he arrived. He didn't look all that surprised to see me. Maybe he thought I merely wanted the loan of one of his men. I didn't waste his time. As soon as I was in his office I told him why I was there.

"You remember a few years ago lending me a Geoff Templett for a certain job?"

"That's right," he said. "I did. Why do you ask?"

"And didn't he leave you a week or two later and go to America?"

"He did. To New York. I remember I had a letter from him."

"Well, I'm pretty sure I saw him in Regent Street yesterday afternoon. If it wasn't, it was the very spit of him, except for a moustache."

"You probably did," he told me amusedly. "He's been back here about a year."

"He has?"

"I thought you might know," he said, "or maybe you don't keep track of all the mushroom agencies that keep springing up."

"You mean he's started his own agency?"

"That's right What's the name of the street, now. Ah! Wentmore Street, just off Shepherd's Market. Calls it simply Confidential Enquiries, Limited. Quite a nice place, I believe."

"Who makes up the Limited?"

He shrugged his shoulders. "Don't know. He uses a couple of operatives and I think his brother's in with him."

"I didn't know he had a brother."

He smiled. "Oh, he has a brother all right. Two or three years older. Used to run a second-hand car mart. Priory Road, Bethnal Green. I wanted a car for the business and Geoff recommended him to me. A tricky customer. I bought the car but I dropped him like a hot potato."

"Why?"

"Well, he specified cash and not a cheque. That was okay with me but the car cost me three hundred and fifty. He wanted to give me a receipt for five hundred. Said it'd help with income tax."

I grunted. "I see. But had the brother—Geoff—anything like that in him?"

"Not that I ever ran across. He was always straight enough with me. And quite a good worker. You found him all right, didn't you?"

"As far as I remember," I said. "In fact I'm pretty sure I did. There was only just one thing: when he was leaving. I think I was thanking him and suddenly he began quite a speech. If you remember, we didn't have to finish that case he was on. Nobody's fault: just one of those things, but he began telling me how he reckoned he'd let me down and how, up till then, he'd thought he knew his job, and now he wasn't so sure, and how bungling things had taught him a lesson. It struck me at the time as utterly insincere. Right out of character."

Tom was looking a bit incredulous. "That was queer. What the devil was he up to?"

"I think I've just got it," I told him. "I remember he ended his little speech by saying he now knew he ought to have more experience. Wasn't it very shortly afterwards that he left you?"

"About a fortnight. He couldn't leave before without breaking his contract."

There was something else that seemed peculiar.

"Sorry to keep labouring the point, Tom, but why should he have to hint to me that he was going to leave *you*! What was it to do with me? And why all that maudlin palaver? As I see it now, he was playing some sort of game."

"He knew the job couldn't be finished?"

"Certainly. But I'd assured him it was through no fault of his own."

"Don't know," he said. "What if he really thought you were going to give me a pretty poor opinion of him?"

"Let's forget it," I told him. Then I think I smiled a bit ruefully. "One thing he did say was that his ambition had been to have his own agency. Maybe that was something else he was trying to work up to. But what I've been working up to myself, Tom, is something I urgently want some information about. Highly confidential information. Do you recall by any chance a boxer named Gannon—Pat Gannon—and how his wife divorced him after a couple of years of marriage? Her name was Caroline. She used to be a model."

He frowned. He was still frowning as he got to his feet and went to the far corner. He began going through a filing cabinet.

"You remember the exact year?"

"I'm pretty sure it was '59."

He tried the bottom drawer and almost at once found what he wanted. It didn't look to me too thick a file and in a minute or so he was replacing it.

"I don't know how you guessed," he said, "but we handled the case for Mrs. Gannon." He held up a hand. "Don't ask me. You're dead right about that, too. Templett was the operative."

"He made a good job of it?"

He came back to his chair.

"A really good job. He finally arranged for this Mrs. Gannon to have to go away for a weekend, but he had her and a friend of hers nice and handy. When Gannon brought a girl to their flat that night, Templett was on the spot. The wife let herself in and she and the friend caught the couple in the act. Templett managed to take a beautiful photograph."

"A nicely baited trap," I said. "And now I'll tell you something, Tom: also highly confidential. I came here on a hunch. Yesterday I saw Templett with the former Mrs. Gannon in Regent Street and I wondered how the two could have got acquainted. Now I know. The lady, by the way, is involved in a case we're handling at the moment."

"You'd hardly believe it," he said. "The world's a mighty small place."

I thought of something else as I moved towards the door. "Have you actually seen Templett?"

"As a matter of fact, I have," he said. "He dropped in about a month or two after he got back. He said he'd done pretty well with a New York agency and had just opened up on his own. Wanted to know if he could borrow a man if he ever wanted one."

"How'd he seem to you?"

"Don't know," he said. "Now I come to think of it, not all that good. I think he'd dropped in to show me he could do a damn sight better elsewhere than with me."

"Local boy makes good," I said. "Wonder why he opened up at that end of town. Most of us are here in the City."

He smiled. "Maybe he's hoping for a better class trade."

"Well, good luck to him," I said, and held out my hand. "Nice of you to've helped me like this."

As I was to tell Hallows, everything had seemed to explain itself. Templett had made the lady's acquaintance when working on her divorce and later the two had almost certainly had an affair. When he had returned he'd tried to pick up where he'd left off but the lady wasn't willing. And meanwhile, she'd married.

I told him about my call on the Daunts. A pretty badly assorted couple, I thought.

"There's that question of a boy-friend," he said. "Assuming Templett wasn't simply guessing. If there is a boyfriend, then maybe Daunt has his suspicions. That might account for various things you saw and heard last night," He looked up. "You still don't think it'd pay to put a tail on her?"

"Only if we had an idea the boy-friend might have been the one who effected the change of the jewellery. Why not let things run on for a bit and hope for a break?"

As a matter of fact we just didn't have a man available for what was bound to be a long surveillance of Caroline Daunt. After the experience and the warnings of the previous afternoon, I doubted if she'd venture to put a foot wrong—at least for quite a time. What I did think we might get on with was a probing into Alan Cofield's alibi.

One of the good things about working for a concern like United Assurance is that you're not pestered for results. If there was no faith in you and your methods, then you wouldn't be employed. Sometimes, of course, there has to be a deadline. This luckily wasn't the case in the matter of the Crewe jewellery. The Crewe estate was hardly likely to be settled for at least another six weeks and even then the jewellery was a personal matter between United Assurance and Julia Crewe. Hill, of course, might be considering a counter-claim for negligence against the firm of John Parwell: a claim he couldn't even begin to think of seriously till we'd provided some facts. It would in any case all be very discreet: decided not in the courts but over a cup of coffee at Lombard Street or Saffron Row.

There wasn't a single party in the affair who didn't want at all costs to avoid publicity, which was why we were handling it and not the police. The Yard's resources are almost unlimited. Every likely maker of keys could have been questioned, for instance, and the private affairs of every suspect exhaustively examined. All we could do was nose along in our own well-tried way and hope for the breaks.

But even if we'd had the available men, we still wouldn't have enquired about keys. There was only one entry to No. 5, Saffron Row. That was by the street door, and it had been furnished with a modern, burglar-proof lock. It hadn't been tampered with because it was tamper proof. The lock of the small safe hadn't been tampered with either, though that was less important. But surely, you may think, I'm presenting an argument in favour of the firm's keys having been used to make copies?

We didn't think so. A special key was required for the burglar-proof lock and to have had a copy made of it would have needed special skills. And whoever used it didn't know that the jewellery substitution would be enquired into privately. He, or she, would have had to face the fact that the Yard would be called in, and risks correspondingly great. No: what we were assuming—at least till we were proved wrong—was that the keys used had been those in the possession of Daunt. That Bendale had a key to the small safe didn't matter. The thief wouldn't have obtained keys from two different people.

At the moment Alan Cofield was the one in whom we were most interested. There was the fact that he had surreptitiously tried to make it entirely Julia Crewe's idea to have the jewellery cleaned, and that he had contrived to be present when it was handed over to Bendale. And now consider something else: something very vital. *The fact that he was in Daunt's office when the jewellery was handed over was enough to give him important information as to into which safe the jewellery had been put.*

If, of course, it had been put into the larger safe, then the question of a key wouldn't have come into it. It would be a question of knowing the combination, and that was a mighty big question indeed. It was something about which Daunt would have to be closely questioned when the time seemed ripe. That might have been in a day or two if it hadn't been that Daunt rang us that very morning, just when Hallows and I were getting down to work.

"I thought you might like to know," he began in his pontifical way, "that I shall be away for two or three days from Sunday next. There are various matters that have to be attended to in Edinburgh."

He must have changed his plans. When I'd left him on the Tuesday afternoon it was with the impression that his visit wouldn't be necessary for quite a few days.

"Nice of you to let us know," I told him. "By the way, there's some information you can give us and save a call on you. It's occurred to you, of course, that on Saturday morning the jewellery might have been put in the large safe, in which case whoever made the substitution would have had to know the combination. Do you often change the combination?"

"Not very often. When it happens to occur to me. Might be six months: might be a year."

"And you keep a record?"

He snorted. "I'd look a pretty fool if I had to open that safe and had forgotten the combination."

"Where do you keep the record?"

"I keep two," he said. "I'm a careful man, Mr. Travers. I keep one in a locked drawer of my desk and the other's always in my wallet. That way there's no possible chance of any accident."

I told him he was a wise man, thanked him and rang off. It took me only a second or two to realise the importance of what I'd just been told.

"He carried the combination on him," I said. "He also carried the keys on him—the one to the door and the one to the small safe. Who was the only one who could have handled the keys and known the safe combination?"

"Plain as the nose on your face," Hallows said. "His wife."

I wondered if they occupied the same bedroom. And if, when he put on a different suit, he was careful to transfer all his belongings.

"Let's jump ahead," Hallows said. "They'd be no use to her personally. She'd have to transfer them to the one who made the substitution. I don't see how that could have been Cofield. We've no information that the two knew each other."

"I don't know," I said. "It's worth enquiring into. But let's get on with Cofield's alibi. What's the best way to start?"

"I'd try Mrs. Crewe," he said. "We have to know where he was after leaving Saffron Row on the Saturday."

So I rang Pentlow House. Robert found Julia Crewe for me and brought her to the telephone.

"Sorry to bother you, Mrs. Crewe, but we ought to have certain things for the records. And treat everyone alike. What I mean is, you heard us question Mr. Daunt and Mr. Bendale about their alibis for the weekend, and we think we ought to have the same information from the rest of you concerned."

"But of course," she said. "Just what is it you want to know?"

"Something highly confidential," I said. "Not about you. About your cousin Alan."

"I see," she spoke quite gravely. "In confidence."

"In confidence. Nothing to do with you personally. We know—I repeat, know—that you had nothing whatever to do with this affair except to be the victim. The other person's different. There are certain discrepancy statements and we're trying to reconcile them or else enquire into them further. By the way, the strict confidence doesn't include your husband: indeed I'd be grateful if you'd tell him privately everything we say."

She told me all she knew. She was shrewd. She knew precisely what was involved in enquiring into an alibi.

Alan Cofield, she could swear, had never been out of her sight from the moment he'd arrived at Pentlow House on the Saturday morning in his sports' car, till he'd left again on the Sunday morning. The call at Saffron Row, lunch, the matinée: he was always there. They took the six o'clock to Chesham and—still in his car—drove back to Pentlow House. He stayed to dinner. Two neighbours, a Colonel Holland and his wife, also came to dinner and bridge. Cofield slept at Pentlow House and left in the morning at half-past nine. He said he was playing in a club competition. That was all she knew.

"Just one other thing, Mrs. Crewe, and it's most important. I ask you to think back very carefully. Disregard for the moment the matter of who first suggested the jewellery ought to be cleaned. What I'd like to be sure about was who first suggested that day in town."

It didn't take her more than a second or two to remember. "Alan did. As soon as it was agreed to have the jewellery examined, he suggested the whole thing. He was most enthusiastic. We'd happened to mention a particular play the previous day and he said why shouldn't we go to the Saturday matinee. He was very persuasive. Before I hardly knew where I was, the whole thing was arranged."

I made no comment: merely thanked her. "And thank you again for giving us such a lovely day."

She told me quietly that the pleasure had been theirs. As soon as the unhappy matter in hand had been cleared up, we must come again.

What we'd learned seemed most important.

"What about your going down to Hollindale and ferreting round to see what happened to Cofield between ten on the Sunday and nine the next morning?"

"Why not give Cofield the chance to tell us himself?" he said. "Ring him now. It might save a journey."

I hardly expected to find Cofield in, but I did. I tried the same gambit as with Julia Crewe, only this time with special emphasis on the fiction that Daunt had been annoyed that only he and Bendale had been questioned about alibis. The reason Cofield was in, by the way, was that he was thinking of going to Pentlow House. I hoped to heaven the Crewes wouldn't display the least frigidity.

"I had to get back before ten," he said, "because it was the monthly medal. I had lunch with my partner at the club-house and then we had a foursome in the afternoon. Just managed to finish before dusk. After dinner four people came in and we played poker till just after midnight. One of them was the club secretary, Major Lovell. Then I went to bed. Slept like a log. Between you and me, old boy, I was sound asleep when Mary brought a cup of tea in at nine o'clock."

"That's all right," I told him. "Just a formality. And it gives Daunt no cause for complaint."

I was wondering how to ring gracefully off, when he put a question. "Tell me something, old boy: just between ourselves, what do you think of that fellow Daunt?"

"To tell the truth, I hardly know him."

"But didn't you think he was far too touchy? And what about his business? For all we know he might be on the rocks."

I told him it was worth bearing in mind. I think he wanted to go on, but I told him someone was wanting to speak to me on another line.

Hallows had been listening in.

"The trouble with him is, he talks too much," he said. "I have an idea he might dig his own grave."

"I think you should go down there," I said. "Somehow I can't get away from the idea that the answer's to be found outside town. It's somewhere in that fairly tight circle: the Crewes at Pentlow House, Cofield at Hollindale and Caplin somewhere between. If the jewellery was brought from there, so to speak, then surely the replicas were too."

"You might be right," he said. "It'll be a bit tricky but it might be managed. And it's all only about thirty or so miles from town."

He'd probably heard it before but I told him something which Jewle had once told me. Detective-Superintendent Jewle of New Scotland Yard is a very old friend of mine. In the old days—he was only a sergeant then—I actually worked with him on quite a number of cases. When my real contacts ceased with the Yard, he'd already moved up to inspector.

What he'd happened to tell me, in some context that I've forgotten, was that when he was a sergeant working on a case with a chief-superintendent, there'd been something so trivial that he hadn't bothered to enquire into it. Later, that triviality had turned out to be something highly important.

"I kept my mouth shut and hoped for luck," he'd told me, "and luckily I slipped through the mesh. You know what would have happened if the Old Man had known I'd had that clue in my possession? He'd have broken me, just like that. Do you know I still sometimes think of it and go all of a sweat. Ever since then there's no such thing with me as a triviality."

Later that morning after Hallows had gone I was hoist in a way with my own petard. Bertha had brought in coffee and I'd got my pipe going and was leaning back comfortably in one of the easy chairs we have for clients, and going over the morning's happenings. I believe I had my eyes shut.

Something or other brought Templett to my mind and I switched my thoughts to him. I was soon stirring uneasily. I felt that I wanted to know a whole lot more about him. Maybe I ought to pay a friendly visit to that bright new agency of his. Then I didn't like the idea, but it made me wonder somehow about the agency for whom he'd worked in New York. It couldn't surely, by a million to one chance, be the McGuffie Agency? They're our New York agents. A million to one was an exaggeration. The chances lay with the number of reputable agencies, but the number of those I couldn't begin to guess. In any case the idea was preposterous. I glanced at my watch, drank the rest of my coffee and hoisted myself up from the chair. It was then, for some reason or other, that I remembered again that experience of Jewle's: the one I'd related only a few minutes before to Hallows.

I asked Bertha to come in. I scribbled a few ideas on a pad and dictated a letter to be sent at once by air-mail to the McGuffie Agency. I wanted confidential enquiries made about a Geoff Templett, said to have worked from about 1959 to 1962 for a New York agency. I gave the fullest possible description and added that up to the time he'd left England he'd been employed as an operative by the Jordan Agency, whom he—McGuffie—knew.

7

MISSING LADY

HALLOWS wouldn't be back, I thought, for at least a day—it might even be two—so the Crewe case went into the background. It popped out again that evening when I was watching a television play, the main plot of which was built round an alibi. It set me thinking about Cofield.

I couldn't help thinking how very amenable he had been when we'd rung him about his alibi: never an objection, never a hesitation. Even if he had a naturally co-operative nature and a desire to please at least those among whom he was prepared to move socially, I somehow couldn't find altogether natural the promptness and even the amiability with which he had told me about that alibi. It hadn't been natural even when one considered that, for him, being an eager beaver and always only too happy to oblige had brought both pleasure and profit for a good many years of his life.

It was, in fact, as if he'd been expecting some sort of enquiry into his alibi and had therefore had the whole thing ready. And there was another thing. He could have given just the bare bones: said, for instance, that on the Sunday night he'd played poker with some friends. But he hadn't kept it to that. He'd mentioned the name of one of them—the club secretary, a Major Lovell, whom, one could assume, he was practically inviting us to question. And since I had also to assume that the major concerned couldn't be a party to the faking of an alibi, there seemed only one conclusion to draw. Alan Cofield's alibi was perfectly good. During the whole of the vital hours he'd been where he'd said he'd been, and nowhere else.

Excuse my labouring the point, but I had to try to get the whole thing thrashed out. I'm not snobbish: in fact I hate snobbery. I don't announce or even admit to all and sundry that I was at such-and-such a school and such-and-such a

Cambridge college. If those facts happen to come out—well, they come out. All the same, I speak good standard English and I assume I have quite the normal good manners: what I mean is that Cofield should very soon have recognized—as I think he did recognise—that I was someone of his own social class.

When, then, I asked for his alibi, his reply should have been something like this. "I don't know what you're getting at, old boy, but you know me. That jewellery business didn't do me any good. I'm one of the family."

And so on till my insistence brought a brief alibi. But it hadn't been like that at all. To sum the whole thing up, Cofield had a genuine alibi because, for some reason of his own, it was highly important that he should have one. In other words, while he knew how the substitution had been worked and had helped to create a suitable situation, it was essential for him to be in a position to prove that he couldn't have had any possible hand in it.

In the morning those overnight ruminations had a definite confirmation of still more fact. Hallows rang me from his home soon after nine and said he was just off to Buckinghamshire again. As soon as he began telling me what had happened the previous afternoon, I knew he'd been thinking along the same lines as myself.

Cofield hadn't been to Pentlow House or, if he had, he hadn't stayed to lunch. Hallows had lunched at the Angel, the local hotel, and had contrived to pick up Cofield and a partner on the fourth tee. Cofield had looked surprised. Hallows told him he was due for a week's holiday very soon and was thinking he might do worse than spend it playing golf. He'd just lunched at the Angel and had liked it there. Did the club have a sort of composite green fee for, say, a week?

Cofield introduced him to his partner as an old friend.

"Mind if I walk along with you for a few holes? I'd like to get the lie of the land."

"Do, old boy, do," Cofield told him, so Hallows followed the pair round. He'd played the game for a short time when he was a younger man, so he wasn't an absolute fool, and he also made himself useful by taking on Cofield's trolley. The golf was very good and Hallows stayed on till the end of the round. The three might have known each other for years by the time they'd finished tea in the club-house. Then the partner had to leave.

A minute or two and Cofield had a bit of luck. The club secretary came into the lounge and Hallows was introduced. Cofield gave Hallows a surreptitious dig in the ribs.

"Just the man I wanted to see. Bob Hallows here, reckoned he saw me somewhere in town on Sunday night and I bet him half-a-crown he didn't. You tell him, Jim."

Hallows was duly told. Cofield chuckled and held out a hand for the half-crown.

"Cofield's smarter than I gave him credit for," I said. "Wonder where he learned that little trick."

"Probably on television. But this was what was so curious. I hadn't mentioned that alibi of his. I hadn't even mentioned the case. All I was at Hollindale for was fixing up a golfing holiday, yet as soon as Major Lovell came into the room, he was bolstering up his alibi. When he went with me to the car I asked him what it had all been about: pretended I knew nothing about your wanting his alibi. He looked, or tried to look, quite surprised."

Cofield, I said, was throwing that alibi at us. He wanted it challenged because he knew it would hold.

"What's your idea of him now?" I said.

"I think he knows how the stunt was pulled. Perhaps he helped to organise it. It's even possible that part of it depended on his having an alibi. I'm still trying to fit it all in."

I asked him what he was thinking of doing, and he said he might call at Pentlow House during the morning, but only if he could think up a good excuse. If not he would call on Caplin who might have remembered something else about the replicas.

Something occurred to me just as I was about to ring off.

"By the way, Bob, did Cofield give you that half-crown back?"

He chuckled. "You bet he did. I wouldn't have let him get away with that."

"You had to ask him for it?"

"I don't think I did," he said. "I remember I was going to mention it and then he handed it over. Why do you want to know?"

I said I was trying, as it were, to recreate the scene.

I settled down to routine work and ended the morning with a conference with Norris. I'd just got back from a late lunch when Hallows rang. He said he'd just had lunch at the Grapes at Newhurst. Would I do something for him.

"It's to do with women's magazines," he said. "Am I right in thinking there're only two main groups? If it's as easy as that, I'd like to know if any magazine under their control employs a woman named Eleanor Morse. Just that. I'll carry on from there as soon as I know."

He might have been talking gibberish for all the sense it made to me. I told him I'd do what I could. He said he'd be in before five and then he rang off.

I did some verification from the reference books, then I talked things over with Norris. Then we got busy, each using a line. I don't know which of us had the more exasperating couple of hours. The very mention of a detective agency was enough to raise the suspicions of a listener. My objective was the personnel manager, and you'd have thought I was coming for him with a hand-grenade. It also turned out that most of those magazines were partially autonomous, and finally I was told that I'd be rung back. I consulted Bertha, then rang

Bernice, and between them they gave me the names of the three magazines with what they thought would be the largest circulation. Norris and I ignored all that had gone before and began again with a direct approach. We found people to talk to, only to be asked why the information was wanted. We said it was a matter of a legacy, and we'd been asked to find an Eleanor Morse, the legatee, who was last heard of in the employ of an important women's magazine.

Even the blandishment of that word important produced only partial results. None of the magazines knew anything about any such person. We were still digging away at a quarter to five when Hallows turned up. He seemed astonished at the furore he'd caused.

"You should have rung So-and-So," he told us. "I'll ring him myself as soon as I've told you what it's all about."

The story was this. That morning he'd inadvertently over shot that side lane to Newhurst but he'd kept on towards Chesham, thinking there'd soon be another. About three miles on he'd found one and, by the direction post, Newhurst was five miles away. The lane was narrower than the one we'd taken, and about a mile along it a car was approaching—a fairly old Rolls. He'd drawn across on the actual verge and it was just as the Rolls was passing him that he happened to notice that Julia Crewe was driving, with her husband beside her. Neither had apparently recognised him: if they had he thought they'd have pulled up. As he drove on, he knew there was now no need for an excuse to see the Crewes or for the call at Pentlow House. What he could do was have a chat with Robert. There was nothing special he hoped to unearth: still, one never knew.

Robert Lockyer, the butler, was almost apologetic about the absence of the Crewes. They were calling on some old friends, he said, but he expected them back well before lunch.

"But come in sir. It's cold this morning, sir. Looks as if we're in for a change."

He ushered Hallows into the room in which we'd spent best part of a morning. "You'd like some coffee, sir?"

He stirred the fire. "You want a good fire mornings like these, sir. There's a copy of *The Times* there, sir, if you don't happen to have seen it."

It was about ten minutes before he came back with a tray. "Your coffee, sir. I hope it'll be to your liking."

"There's something I've been thinking," Hallows said. "But sit down a minute, if you're not busy. What car does Mrs. Crewe drive?"

"A Rolls, sir. It was the master's originally, sir, but her ladyship hardly used it at all after he died, and then when Mr. David arrived, he had it overhauled for Miss Julia to drive."

Hallows mentioned the curious meeting in the lane. Robert was again apologetic. Miss Julia had probably had her eyes on the road, he said. She'd certainly have stopped if she'd recognised him.

Hallows tried to steer the talk in the direction of Alan Cofield. He'd wanted to know just what rôle he'd played during the widowhood of Lady Crewe. All he got was that her ladyship had been very fond of him and, in lighter vein, that it was always helpful to have a man about the house.

"But she still managed everything pretty well herself?"

"Most certainly, sir. Her ladyship, if I may say so, sir, was a most capable lady in every way. And quite a famous one, sir."

He broke off. There was something he was remembering. It came back to him almost at once. "I wonder if you can tell me something, sir. Pardon the question, but are you married?"

"Indeed I am."

"Then if Mrs. Hallows happens to take any of the women's magazines, did you by any chance see an article on her ladyship?"

"Not that I remember. If there had been one I think I'd have spotted it."

"Very strange, sir." He shook his head. "I saw our news-agent and asked him to look out for it. Also I ought to have been sent a copy. I just can't understand it, sir."

"Understand what?"

And so to the story. Lady Crewe died in the early hours of a Monday morning. Robert rang the solicitors who sent obituary notices to the leading newspapers and got into touch with the Crewes. The London evening papers carried the obituary notices, as did the papers of the Tuesday morning. The Crewe's couldn't arrive till the early afternoon of the Wednesday, but the solicitors had everything in hand. A member of the firm had spent the Tuesday morning at Pentlow House but he hadn't stayed to lunch. Robert and the housekeeper were alone in the house that afternoon.

At about half-past two the front door-bell was rung. A woman was there, asking to see a member of the family. Robert explained.

"Then perhaps you could help me," she said. "My name's Eleanor Morse and I've been commissioned by my magazine to write a special article on Lady Crewe. We have the main features of her life, but we'd like to fill in certain details in view of her death. May I come in?"

Robert stood his ground. "What magazine would that be, madam?"

Unfortunately he didn't quite catch the name but it did have the word "woman" in it. Hallows suggested various names but none of them seemed to be exactly right.

"Naturally you'll be sent a copy," she was going on. "May I have your name?"

She produced a notebook, but just at that moment something happened. Who should be coming along the drive but Alan Cofield in his car. Robert told the journalist who Cofield was and said she might prefer to mention her business to him. She was in such a hurry to do so that she forgot to thank him.

Cofield *must* have seen her coming. He drew his car up at the far end of the house, and the last that Robert saw was Cofield getting out of the car as the woman came up.

"You mentioned the matter to Mr. and Mrs. Crewe?"

"Yes, sir. But not till after the funeral. She seemed rather annoyed, sir. She said she'd see Mr. Alan about it."

"How long was Mr. Alan with the woman? Do you know?"

"I couldn't say, sir. I know it was at least a half-hour before he came in."

"And you never saw the woman again?"

"No, sir. I'd given her my name, but I never received a copy of anything she wrote."

"What exactly was she like? Can you describe her?" Hallows, like me as I listened, had expected a someone resembling Caroline Daunt. That would have given us a connection between Caroline and Cofield, but it was nothing of the sort. I'd been idiotically optimistic even to think of it: it had about it too much melodrama. Eleanor Morse had been a woman of barely medium height and on the plump side. She'd had light brown—almost blond—hair which she wore cut straight along the line of her neck. Her complexion was what Robert called reddish, and she was wearing dark glasses. He put her age at getting on for forty.

"Tell you what I'll do," Hallows had told him. "I know a lot of people in Fleet Street so I'll make enquiries. If I run the woman down I'll find out why she didn't send you a copy of the magazine."

Robert seemed most grateful, and in a minute or two Hallows left. At the door he put another question or two.

"Do you know if Mr. Cofield mentioned the matter to Mrs. Crewe?"

Robert had assumed that he'd been going to do so.

"And Mrs. Crewe never mentioned it to you?"

She hadn't.

Hallows drove on to Hollindale and the hotel. It was about half-past eleven and he still hadn't thought out a method of approach to Cofield. Then he caught sight of him in the bar. Cofield hadn't seen him so he slipped back to the desk and booked a room for a fortnight's time. He came back to the bar, ordered a pint and allowed Cofield to spot him.

"Good God! What're you doing here, old boy? Living here?"

Hallows explained that he'd had to call at Pentlow House and had taken advantage of the call to drive on to the hotel and book a room for his holiday. He stood Cofield a gin and French and moved back from the bar to a table.

"The Crewes were out," he told Cofield, "But Robert insisted on making me some coffee. Which reminds me. He told me a rather curious story."

And so to the visit of Eleanor Morse. Cofield hadn't actually been hit clean in the wind, but there'd been a second or so at the deliberately abrupt mention of her name when he'd been taken very much aback. Then he'd laughed the whole thing off.

"I remember her, old boy. Looked like a she-beatnik. A bit cool, don't you think, under the circumstances?"

"You sent her off with a flea in her ear?"

"I certainly did. In double-quick time. I wasn't actually rude, mind you, but I had to let her see she wasn't wanted. As I told her, there'd been a book or two written about my aunt, and, if she wanted information, let her look them up."

Hallows congratulated him. It had been just the way to handle a Fleet Street ghoul.

"What did Mrs. Crewe think about it?"

According to Cofield, she'd heartily agreed with the line he'd taken. And that was virtually that. Hallows had claimed to have urgent business and had left. As he was in the neighbourhood he'd called at Bertram Caplin's place and found him out. Then he'd circled round to Newhurst village and had had a scratch lunch at the pub. Then he'd rung me. After that he'd rung a friend in Fleet Street and was told he'd not be along till six. He hadn't really expected to get into touch with him but he did expect to find him at home. He drove to Norwood, only to find him out. A spot of tea at a Norwood tea-shop and he'd driven on to Broad Street.

"What's the actual importance of it all?" I asked him.

"You tell me," he said. "I'm going on quite a few things. Cofield claimed to've got rid of the woman in double-quick time. Robert said it was over half an hour. And Cofield was talking with her all that time and didn't bring her into the house. Then there was the expression on Cofield's face when I mentioned her in the hotel. Also that indignation of his didn't ring true. And his description of the woman. She wasn't any kind of beatnik. She had bobbed hair but Robert said she spoke quite well and was quite well dressed. And, of course, there's the apparent fact that she didn't write any article. You don't tell me that a woman journalist who's been commissioned to write a special article is going to be put off as easily as that."

I was just telling him that he certainly seemed to have it all worked out, when the buzzer went. A somebody-or-other was telling us that they didn't appear to have the information we required. Hallows said he'd get along to Fleet Street. With any luck he'd know by the morning anything about Eleanor Morse that was worth the knowing. I wasn't sorry to call it a day.

It wasn't till the Saturday morning that he was sure about the woman who'd called that morning at Pentlow House.

No woman's magazine of the kind at all likely to wish to publish an article on Lady Crewe had even heard of an Eleanor Morse. None of Hallows's acquaintances or connections in Fleet Street had the slightest knowledge of her, nor was it thought that a journalist of the kind she'd described herself would have needed to employ any subterfuges. Lady Crewe had been at one time a national figure and, even if a generation or more had arisen that knew not Joseph, it wouldn't have been inapt that on her death some magazine readers should be reminded of her. Hallows smiled dryly when he told me that at least a couple of editors had shown signs of exasperation at having missed that particular boat.

There was just the chance, of course, that Eleanor Morse had been a freelance, but, if so, her name should surely have been found in the telephone directory. A telephone, Hallows said, was the freelance's main artery. There was something else about her that he felt he ought to explore. Eleanor Morse had arrived at Pentlow House, but how? By train to somewhere and on by taxi? He couldn't even guess but it had seemed a promising opening. To know how she had come might be a chance to trace her back.

If she had arrived by taxi, it would have driven up to the front door and the butler would have seen it and, if so, mentioned it. Hallows wasn't sure about that, but he thought it might be worth while to ring. It was Robert who happened to answer the phone.

"Sorry I forgot to mention it when we were talking about it, sir, but she came by car. I don't know why, sir, but she left it out of sight at the bend. A man who was working in the gardens heard her drive up and saw her get out and go towards the house."

Except that the man thought the car was fairly old and the colour black, that was all that could be learned.

"Maybe she was ashamed of driving an old car up to the front door of the house," I said. "She might have thought it a loss of face."

"No journalist ought to be ashamed of driving an old car these days," he said. "When you add it to what we know and don't know, I think she left it there so that no one should happen to remember the number."

I thought things over for a moment or two and decided to put a categorical question.

"You really think this woman is tied up somehow with the jewellery business?"

"I do. I honestly do. I'd like to go back there on Monday morning—to Newhurst, that is—and find out if she was seen in the village. She almost certainly had to come that way, so she might have asked someone the way to the house. It's a good half-mile away."

That was how we left things. I spent a quarter of an hour with John Hill, bringing him up to date before, like the rest of us, he began a well-earned weekend. By bed-time on the Sunday night I don't suppose I'd thought about the case more than once or twice, and then only casually. I remember I did wish it was I who was going to Newhurst in the morning. There was quite a lot of mist about that night but the weather forecast had promised a clear day.

What I could never have guessed was that there'd be no day for either of us in the Buckingham countryside. Nine in the morning wouldn't even find me at Broad Street. I'd be with Jewle at the Yard.

8

JEWLE HAS A THEORY

AT SEVEN o'clock on that Monday morning I was just lying comfortably in bed and knowing complacently that I could do so for another quarter of an hour. That's when I get up, put on my glasses and a dressing-gown and trudge off to our small kitchen to make early morning tea. A second or two after seven the telephone went. Who could be calling me at that hour, and at my private address, I couldn't imagine. In fact, I thought it must be a wrong number.

It wasn't. It was Jewle. I spotted his voice almost as soon as he spoke. "That you, Mr. Travers?"

"Jewle, isn't it?"

"That's right. You think you could oblige us by coming along straight away? Are you dressed?"

I said I wasn't but I soon could be. He said a car would call for me in a quarter of an hour, and then he rang off. I wouldn't in any case have asked what it was all about. I'd have been wasting my time.

I'd rather expected him to be in the car that I found waiting for me, but he wasn't. There was so little distance to go that I wondered why he'd sent a car at all. I can walk from my St. Martin's flat to the Yard in six minutes if I'm pushed for time. When we drew in, the driver said the Super would be joining me, and we just waited. Five minutes and Jewle came bustling across. He said he much appreciated everything, though what everything was I didn't yet know.

We were heading west before he began telling me. "You know a jeweller named Daunt?"

"I do," I said. "He's one of the interested parties in a case we're still working on for United Assurance. Why d'you want to know?"

"Because his body was found this early morning at Harrow. Lying in a side road just off the main street. He had one of your cards in his pocket."

It takes quite a deal these days to put me at a loss, but what he'd told me so bluntly really shook me.

"Everybody concerned in the case had one of our cards," I said. "They'd want our telephone number in case there was anything to ring up about."

"Of course," he said, with just a touch of placation.

You can't ruffle Jewle. Like most really big men he's quiet and easy-going. He could have had the old Latin tag as a family motto—the one about suave in manner but tough when it came to the point.

"You'd like to tell me about it?"

"You tell me something first," I said. "Is this a question of murder?"

"In all probability, yes."

If it had been anything less I'd have temporised till I saw how things were shaping. Murder's a different matter. The quicker you come clean, the better for all concerned. All the same there was no risk great in under-playing my hand. I wanted to spin things out: to make myself time.

Jewle knows John Hill almost as well as I do. Various cases in which United Assurance have been concerned have necessitated calling in the law.

"Just one of those routine cases," I said. "Missing jewellery. It disappeared from Daunt's premises during the weekend November the second to the fourth. John Hill called us in."

"Then you knew Daunt?"

I could have told him a whole lot of things, but I didn't. What I'd decided was to dispense in driblets, hoping there'd soon be no more questions to ask. I said that naturally I'd known him. I'd had to see him three or four times. Hallows and I had had quite a talk with him at Saffron Row on the afternoon of the fifth.

I've occasionally flattered myself that, when it comes to delaying tactics, Fabius Cunctator might have learned quite a deal from me. Delaying the enemy and protecting a client are pretty much the same thing, but somehow that early morning, sitting there alongside Jewle and with his eyes steadily on me, I wasn't quite so sure. That was why I decided to give a start of surprise.

"Wait a minute. Something's wrong somewhere. You say he was found dead early this morning at Harrow?"

"That's right. At about four o'clock by the man on the beat."

"That's what's wrong," I said. "He rang me only a day or so ago to let me know he wouldn't be available for questioning for a bit."

There was very little traffic and the car had been bowling smoothly along. Harrow's no great distance and I reckoned we'd be there in another few minutes.

"You mean he was going away?" Jewle said.

I asked how much he knew about Daunt, and it turned out to be virtually nothing at all, so I told him practically all I knew about John Parwell—the firm, that is—and the Edinburgh branch. Daunt should have been there instead of lying dead at Harrow.

We were entering Harrow. Jewle was digesting what I'd been telling him and he didn't say another word except to the driver. A couple of minutes and we were taking a side turn. We made a complete U-turn and into another residential side road. Two police cars were there. I spotted an old friend—Jewle's side-kick, Inspector Matthews.

"Would you mind staying here?"

Jewle moved off. I craned out of the window but couldn't see a body. Only two people were there besides Matthews, and Jewle was joining them. I hate to smoke before a meal but I lighted my pipe just to pass the time. A couple of minutes and Matthews was at the open window.

"Hallo, sir? They got you up early, didn't they?"

Matthews is always one for a quip. He said the Old Man thought I might like to see the X that marked the spot. Jewle was alone. One of the cars was driving away and there wasn't any definite spot. Daunt's body had been found lying by the kerb as if it had been tipped out of a car.

"The car mightn't even have stopped," Jewle said. "At that time of the morning no one would have heard anything."

It was a quiet, residential street of semi-detached houses with gardens running back some twenty feet from the road.

"I suppose you've no idea why he should have been here at all?" Jewle asked me.

I said it was inexplicable. As far as I knew he should have been in Edinburgh. He *could* have changed his mind.

The body had long since gone. Matthews would be staying on to organise some local questioning but we, Jewle said, might as well get back to the Yard.

"You say Hallows was working with you on this jewellery business?"

"He was. And is."

"Right," he said. "I'll get you to give him a ring. He ought to be at the Yard by the time we get back." He paused. "On second thoughts, I'll ring him myself if you give me his number."

I tried to make a joke of it. "Why all the suspicion?"

He just smiled quietly and waited for the number.

It was not a lot past eight o'clock when we left the local police-station. The traffic was only just beginning to build up but it was well after nine when we drew in at the Yard. Hallows was waiting in Jewle's room with a youngish detective sergeant for company. He took care not to give me a questioning look.

Hallows, where Jewle is concerned, is also a very old friend. Jewle wanted to know if he'd had breakfast, and he had. I hadn't neither had Jewle. Toast and coffee would be good enough for me, and Jewle rang down for the same for himself. While we were waiting, he said, Hallows could be giving his own version of things generally. He was sure we wouldn't mind if it was a kind of unofficial statement. It was all very friendly and even genial.

"What kind of information is it that you want?" Hallows said.

"Oh, anything you think might help. That jewellery case you've been engaged on, for instance, and just how Daunt was connected. Things like that."

A stenographer followed hard on the heels of the toast and coffee and Hallows began talking. I chewed and drank and put in never a word. Not that I didn't feel a certain apprehension. Hallows left virtually nothing out. What he didn't do was go even a day beyond the opening Tuesday.

"An extraordinary business," Jewle said. "Most extraordinary. And what have you found out since?"

"Virtually nothing," Hallows said. He gave his dry smile. "That's something else that's extraordinary. We've taken quite a lot of time testing the alibis of the four people concerned and can't find a flaw. When we left things on Saturday, we hoped the weekend'd give us some new ideas. Now this has happened."

"Nothing else you can think of, Mr. Travers?"

I said Hallows seemed to have covered everything.

"Yes," Jewle said, but he didn't wave to the stenographer to go. "I think, you know, the whole thing's a pity. Surely Daunt was killed because of something you've been telling us?"

I said I was certainly disposed to think so.

"That's what I mean by it being a pity," Jewle said. "Daunt might still be alive if we'd been called in from the very first."

"Come, come," I told him reprovingly. "That was John Hill's affair. Also, everybody wanted the whole thing kept a sort of family matter. There's nothing contrary to the law in that."

Jewle smiled. "I didn't even hint there was."

He turned to Hallows again. I was glad he did.

"What's Daunt's wife like?"

"Don't know," Hallows said. "I've never even clapped eyes on her. You can't very well ask a wife about her husband's alibi."

"I suppose not."

He thought for a moment, then said that seemed to be about all. If we liked to wait we could check the statements. I said I didn't think it'd be necessary, so the stenographer went. As the door was closing on him, the sergeant came in.

"The possessions, sir, you wanted to see."

There seemed very little and, what there was, was tied up in a clean white handkerchief. Jewle opened it out on his desk. There was a little loose money—about four shillings in all—a pocket knife, a stub of pencil and nothing else.

"No wallet," I said.

"No wallet. No ticket to Edinburgh, no cloak-room ticket for left luggage, nothing but what you see there. And that card of yours. That was in a fob pocket."

I was going to ask if robbery was the murder motive, but I didn't. There was an unreality about everything. If I'd seen Daunt's body lying that morning by the kerb, the dead man himself would have been something real. Somehow I couldn't imagine him there. Every now and again, as when Hallows had been talking, I'd seen him in my mind's eye: Daunt at that Tuesday morning conference: Daunt in his own office and, above all, Daunt in his flat, and somehow those brief recollections merely added to the unreality. And then something occurred to me.

"Nothing but these things here? Then how on earth did you identify him?"

"By luck," Jewle said. "You know those embroidered tapes with your name on that you use on laundry? He had 'em on the back of his shirt. And his vest. His full name—Stephen Daunt. I think you have to pay for up to twelve letters in any case. After that it was only a question of looking in the telephone directory. Half an hour before I called you, I was at the block of flats and getting hold of the superintendent."

Jewle has that trick of stopping at apparently the wrong place: say, the tantalising place. It invites a question. Sometimes it's a question that never ought to have been put: something that incriminates. I don't think he had that in mind for Hallows and me. If he did have anything of the sort, neither of us rose to it.

"As a matter of fact it complicated things," he went on. "Mrs. Daunt was away for the weekend and wasn't due back till tomorrow. Daunt stopped at the desk at about eleven o'clock on the Sunday morning. He was carrying a weekend bag and said he'd probably not be back till Wednesday. It was a rule of the management that flats should never be left empty for over twelve hours without the desk being informed."

"You managed to get into touch with Mrs. Daunt?" Hallows said.

"No. She'd left no forwarding address. Daunt had been away in Edinburgh before."

"There's a suitable train round about noon?"

"Yes," Jewle said. "Edinburgh's undoubtedly where he was bound for. Our problem is, why didn't he go there?"

"Heaven knows," I said.

I had a quick check in my notebook. "If he *had* gone, it'd have been to 71 Rievers Street."

"Right," Jewle said. "Under what name would the number be?"

I suggested John Parwell. He rang instructions through. He was looking a lot more happy as he lighted his pipe.

"You people are being a great help," he told us. "I have an idea we'll have to rely on you quite a deal. I take it John Hill will want you to go on with the case?"

"Why not?" I said. "As far as his company's concerned, Daunt's death doesn't solve his problem. There's best part of fifty thousand pounds at stake."

He raised his eyebrows. "As much as that?"

"Good quality diamonds," I said. "Really high-class stuff."

The buzzer went. He picked up the receiver. A moment or two and I gathered he was through to Edinburgh. He mentioned a name—Weeks—and jotted it down on his pad. There wasn't much else to listen to at his end but it wasn't hard to gather that somewhere something was wrong.

"Right," he said at last. "Thank you, Mr. Weeks. You carry on as usual. No need to get into touch with Mr. Daunt."

He replaced the receiver and for a moment he didn't move. The he looked up. He might have been smiling.

"I think that business of yours may be having some queer complications. You heard me talking to a Mr. Weeks? He says he had no idea Daunt was coming to Edinburgh. What's more, if Daunt had been coming, he'd very definitely have let him know. It was essential he should do so and he always did."

"A bit of a facer," I said. "You got any ideas?"

"Strictly between ourselves—well, I might have."

"Such as?"

"Well, Daunt wasn't bound for Edinburgh. He let you people and his wife think he was, but he was really bound elsewhere."

He gave us a questioning look. Again we didn't rise to it.

"Why not abroad? Suppose, for instance, he was going to dispose of those diamonds?"

Hallows gave a little grunt. "It could be. Mind if I take it from there? Fill in some details?"

"Carry on," Jewle told him. "I'm an interested party."

"Well, starting off with your simple thesis, on Sunday morning Daunt didn't go to King's Cross. He might have gone to Liverpool Street and booked to Harwich or to Charing Cross for Dover. But some other party or parties knew what he'd be carrying and somehow they managed to get hold of him. Later on he was dumped at Harrow so as to give the impression it was just an ordinary robbery. A slugging, shall we say, that turned out wrong."

"It could be," Jewle said. "You got any interested parties in mind?"

"All the interested parties we know of, we've told you already. You may think differently but none of them to my mind fits the bill. That doesn't rule out that someone might have been employed to do the job."

Jewle smiled. "Such as a firm of shady private detectives. I don't know though. I've the feeling we're getting just a little bit out of our depth."

The buzzer went. Jewle reached for the receiver. All I could gather this time was that there was something of which he wanted to be very sure.

"You know," he said, "We can't get away from facts. Thanks in any case."

He hung up. This time he gave a slow shake of the head.

"Well, we're certainly getting a few complications. That was the medical report on Daunt. He had a heart condition and that's what killed him: that and a severe blow on the right temple."

There was nothing we could say.

"Mind you," Jewle went on: "it doesn't affect that theory. Or what we have to do. It may only be the difference between manslaughter and murder."

There seemed nothing much else to say. I began getting to my feet. Jewle said he'd like me to jot down the addresses of anyone who might be concerned, so that they'd be handy. He was really in one of his grateful moods that morning. When he asked what our line of enquiry would be, I simply said that we'd first have to do a bit of digesting. We'd certainly have to see John Hill.

"I think it'll be to both our interests to put all our cards on the table," he told me. "You go on working from your angle and we from ours."

I had to smile. "That sounds uncommonly generous. And what if we should happen to tread on your toes?"

He actually clapped me on the shoulder. "You know me better than that."

"Fine," I said. "We go where we like and question whom we like and when we like, always provided we pass on everything to you. And similarly you tell us anything that might help."

"Just what I had in mind," he said. "Naturally we ought to avoid too much overlapping."

"Most of our suspects have already been seen," Hallows told him. "All we may have to do is watch their reactions to Daunt's death. That leaves them clear for you."

Cerberus accepted the bone. Once more we were thanked and then we left.

"Where to now?" Hallows asked me as we turned into Northumberland Street.

"Don't know," I said. "Let's get ourselves another cup of coffee and talk it over. That little place Jewle and I often go to is just back across the road."

I left him to order while I rang John Hill. The news seemed to rock him back on his heels. He wanted a first-hand report as soon as we could make it. I said we'd try to get to Lombard Street inside an hour.

"A bone to pick with you, young fellow," I said to Hallows as soon as I came back to his table. "Did you really believe that extraordinary theory about Daunt getting slugged by jewel thieves?"

He chuckled. "Did I hell? All I was doing was tagging along. It paid off, didn't it?"

"Paid off how?"

"Well, it made him more amenable. It might have been why he suggested that co-operation business. Far as I remember it's the first time for years we've had a gilt-edged invitation to work with the Yard."

I had to agree, even if I still had a hunch that somewhere there was a catch. I said, if not entirely to the point, that Daunt had definitely been both robbed and slugged.

"I don't know," he said. "At the moment I'm not prepared to accept either. All I accept is that Daunt was found dead in a Harrow road with virtually empty pockets and a badly bruised temple. Talking about him slipping across to Amsterdam or

Paris to dispose of diamonds contradicts everything we know. He owned a prosperous firm with a fine reputation. Jewle's theory was absolute poppycock. I fell in with him to get him off our backs. If he was chasing all those moonbeams, then we'd be left alone to carry on in our own way."

I laughed. "You certainly did a good job. And what now?"

"See John Hill," he said. "Might do worse than spring Jewle's theory on him and watch the reactions. Might learn something from it. You never know."

9
ON A SUNDAY NIGHT

NOTHING much happened that couldn't have been predicted during the half-hour we spent with John Hill. If only to show we were giving good value for money and were right on our toes, I gave him a detailed account of everything that had happened that morning. It left him much less edgy.

Hallows said he ought to know of a theory that had been put to us by Jewle. Hill was horrified. "He couldn't have been serious!"

"You never know with those people," I said. "He may have had his own reasons for putting forward a theory like that. Also you must consider that he wasn't anything like as well informed as we are."

"Well, it's something that's got to be scotched from the very start. It's slanderous. I'll have to have a word with him."

"Don't do that," I said. "Not unless you believe in keeping a dog and barking yourself."

I explained. Let Jewle think what he liked and act accordingly. It would all be confidential and no one would be harmed: unless by a million to one chance there turned out to be something in it. Meanwhile we could go on with enquiries of our own.

"We've got to account for certain things in our own way," Hallows said. "Jewle had certain facts, but he's interpreting them in the wrong way. It'll be up to us to find the right answers. Daunt misled people about his going to Edinburgh, for instance. We have to know why. Jewle didn't have the answer."

Hill said we were right. He added that he'd hardly had his hand off the telephone since he'd heard about poor Daunt. Bendale had been tremendously shocked. Hill had warned him that he might be having a visit from the police and that meanwhile he was simply to carry on.

Julia Crewe had taken the news far more calmly. She'd seemed more perturbed about the actual death than about any possible connection with the jewellery. Hill had assured her that there'd be a continuance of the enquiry and had contrived to ring off. Then he'd rung Cofield but Cofield had been out. Mrs. Froden had said he'd be in for lunch at twelve-thirty so Hill asked for Cofield to ring him back.

It was a quarter past twelve. I suggested we should wait and listen to Cofield's reactions. It might be as well if I took the call myself. And I'd hardly finished speaking when Hill was rung.

"He's on the line," he said, and handed me the receiver.

"Good-morning, Hill," came the jaunty voice. "I'm told you've been ringing me. Sorry I was out."

"As a matter of fact you're talking to Travers," I said. "I'm speaking from Hill's office. There's some news for you."

I waited a moment to let him ask what news, but he didn't.

"Daunt is dead," I said. "Stephen Daunt. The police think he was murdered."

"Good God, no!"

I hadn't a doubt about the shock the news had given him. I heard him take a deep breath.

"This is true? I mean, you're not pulling my leg?"

"I wish I were," I said. "You can take it from me that it's true enough."

"You say—murdered?"

"Yes, murdered. I've had it direct from the police."

"Do you know *where* it was?"

"Not where he was actually killed. His body was found in Harrow, lying in the road."

He didn't speak.

"Thought I'd let you know," I went on. "The police'll be along to question you."

"Me?" He was hunting for words. "Why should they have to question me?"

"Because they already know all about that jewellery business. They have to run down every possible clue. Daunt was one of the parties concerned and so were you. All I'm doing is giving you a tip-off so you'll be ready when they come."

"Thanks," he said heavily. "It was very good of you."

It was he who rang off, and to those last words he hadn't added an *old boy*. In my judgment, what I'd told him had as good as scared him out of his wits.

"How did he take it?" Hill asked as I replaced the receiver.

"Pretty badly," I said. "Naturally it was a shock. Cofield isn't geared to shocks."

"No," he said. "I suppose not."

His buzzer went. This time it was Jewle on the line. We waited while an appointment was made for two o'clock in Hill's office and we were ready to go when Hill hung up.

"You heard that?" he said. "You think you ought to be here?"

It was the last thing we wanted.

"He won't expect it," I said. "Besides, he's already seen us. It's your version of things he wants now."

At Broad Street Norris hadn't been unduly perturbed. Bernice had given my message that Jewle had called me away. He was overdue for lunch, so I took over. I sent out for sandwiches and Bertha made a pot of tea. Hallows was trying to digest something else.

"You really think Cofield was scared?"

"As I told you, I didn't let on to Hill but I was sure of it. Daunt's death should have been just a piece of information."

Hallows is always making—well not precisely unexpected remarks but putting things in an unexpected way. Showing unusual facets, shall we say.

"Sort of what's Hecuba to him or he to Hecuba," he said. "By the way, didn't he throw out hints to you that Daunt had known quite a lot more than he'd admitted?"

"Something of the sort. He might have been trying to throw suspicion. But let's assume he was scared when I told him about Daunt. With the accent on murder. What can we do about it?"

Hallows shrugged his shoulders. "Don't know. Unless we throw him to the lions. Pass the tip on to Jewle."

The buzzer went. It was Jewle—and I hadn't made up my mind about the lions. He said he was just off to see Hill.

"A piece of information you might like to have," he said. "The lab. boys have just finished with Daunt's clothing and the one interesting thing is what they found attached to the bottoms of his trousers. Grass seeds. Even in the turn-ups."

"Good lord!" I said. "Any special kind of seeds?"

"Not if you mean would they help to identify a particular locality. Just ordinary seeds. And tiny burrs. You know the kind of thing."

"I see. Enough to tell you, though, that he'd been in the country. What sort of clothes was he wearing, by the way?"

"Just what he might have been wearing if he'd intended to go to Edinburgh. Good quality worsted suit in a dark grey, a heavy dark overcoat and a black Homburg hat. It was lying against his head when he was found. He also had on dark brown, fur-lined gloves. The gloves had scratches and traces of gravel. We're checking to see if they could have been caused when he was dropped out of a car."

Jewle was in a hurry. He just had time to ask if we had any ideas and then rang off. I was wondering if I ought to have told him about Cofield.

"Just as well to save it," Hallows said. "You never know when we might run short of quids pro quo."

Norris came back. He looked in and went on to his office. Hallows and I were still talking. It was Caroline Daunt about whom we were wondering. If and when she'd see the morning paper. If she'd return at once to the flat. Jewle would have someone waiting for her and we just wondered if we could pick her up before she actually entered Valery House. That was when the buzzer went. Bertha said a Mr. Cofield was on the line.

I told her to put him through. Hallows threw the switch and picked up the other receiver.

"Travers here, Mr. Cofield."

He was off at once in full spate. "Listen, old boy, there's something I want to talk over with you. You do do that sort of thing, don't you?"

"Sorry, but I don't get you. What sort of thing?"

"Well, you're a private detective."

"You mean you want to consult me as a client?"

"That's the idea. There's something I want to talk over with you. I've got to have your advice."

I warned him that if it was anything to do with the jewellery case, I couldn't possibly act. I already had a client—John Hill.

"It isn't that," he said. "It's about—well, something to do with Daunt."

"Daunt personally, or his death, or what?"

He was getting agitated again. "I don't know. It could be about his death."

"You don't want to tell me now?"

"No," he said quickly. "It's—well, it's complicated. Can't you come down here? I can be in from now on." Hallows gave me a nod.

"I suppose I could do," I said. "But we couldn't be with you in under an hour."

He let out a deep breath. "Thanks, old boy. I'll be waiting for you."

He rang off.

"You were right," Hallows said. "He *was* scared. Wonder what the devil it's all about."

I said we'd go and see.

We had to get to the garage to collect my car and it wasn't till half-past three that we got to Hollindale. Cofield must have heard us coming along the short drive: he was waiting at the front porch as we drove up. He was all effusiveness as he ushered us into his lounge. Tea would be ready in a minute.

No tea, I said—not yet. We'd like to hear straightaway whatever it was that he had to tell us. He was thinking things over as he lighted a cigarette.

"I've been thinking," he said. "You've got to assure me that everything's going to be confidential. What I mean is, we don't want anyone else brought in if we can help."

"It will be," I said, "but only on one condition. If it throws light in any way on Daunt's death, then I'll have to pass the information on. If not I'll be in trouble—bad trouble—with the law. I can't take that risk."

He was rubbing his chin as he thought things out. "I see. But I couldn't have had anything to do with his death. I was here all the time."

"Look," I said placatingly. "We've come quite a way because you said you had to tell us something, so why not just tell us?"

"All right," he said suddenly. "I will. You know where the Frodens sleep?"

"Over the garage?"

"That's right. Well, it was on Sunday night about half-past ten. They always turn in about ten or so and Herbert looked out of the window and thought he saw a man, so he put on his trousers and went down. When he got to the bottom of the steps there was a man there, and this man said he'd lost his way and could Herbert direct him to Chesham. When Herbert was sort of thinking it over, he said his name was Daunt. Stephen Daunt!"

I didn't realise at the moment how incredible it was.

"I see," I said, as quietly as I could. "And what did your man do?"

"Well, he'd never heard of a Stephen Daunt but the man looked all right, and there was a lot of mist about and he might have lost his way. He didn't think he was a car thief or anything like that, so he told him the way. The man said his car was on the road at the end of the drive and facing towards Rickmansworth."

"Is Froden handy?" Hallows said. "It might be as well to listen to his story direct."

Cofield got up at once. He must have had Froden parked in the kitchen. I suggested to Hallows he should do the questioning. Froden had never seen Hallows.

If Froden was a bit ill at ease, it was, considering the circumstances, in no more than what one might consider a natural way. When he spoke it was reasonably to the point. When he was questioned there was no hesitation.

"Why did you look out of the window?" Hallows asked him.

"Well, sir, I thought I heard a noise on the gravel, so I got up and looked. I'd only just that minute got into bed."

"You had an idea, when you actually caught sight of him, he might be a car-thief?"

"Yes, sir. I think that's what I thought. I reckoned it was my job to find out what his business was."

"And what was the man like?"

"About my height, sir, near as I can remember."

"About six foot?"

"About that, sir. Not all that big. He spoke like a gentle-man, sir."

"What was he wearing?"

"Some sort of a water-proof, sir. Light-coloured. I think he had a felt hat. And he had a sort of scarf-thing over his mouth: sort of to keep out the cold."

I'd had my eyes on Cofield. He'd watched Froden like the proverbial hawk: ready to come in, maybe, if there was a slip. And now he did come in.

"Tell these gentlemen what else the man said to you. You remember. Just when he went away."

"Yes," Froden said. "He was going away and he asked if I was the owner, and I told him who I was and how Mr. Cofield owned the house. Then he thanked me again and said would I thank the master and I said I'd do so. I said I'd do so straight-away. That was when he gave me a ten-shilling note."

"Froden did ring me," Cofield said. "There's a telephone in case of emergencies. I just couldn't believe my ears. I was in bed."

"Just a minute," I said. "There's a permanent extension to Froden's quarters and at night you have another extension by your bed?"

"That's right. I don't get up usually before nine and there might be something I had to tell him about. Fresh orders or something. It's worked by a switch."

"I've got it. And what exactly did you do?"

"Well, as I said, I couldn't believe my ears. I must have hung up without thinking, and then I sort of wondered what the devil Daunt was doing here, and then I rang Froden. He said he'd thought he'd just heard a car move off. Then I thought I'd go after him in my own car so I slipped some clothes on and got my car out. It was a damn silly idea, so after I'd got through the village I stopped and came back."

I thanked Froden and told him that was all for the moment. Perhaps he'd stand by.

"No wonder you wanted to get into touch with us," I told Cofield. "The whole thing's fantastic. But tell us something. Just what made you suddenly decide to go chasing after Daunt?"

"A sort of impulse, I reckon." He leaned confidentially forward. "You remember what I told you some time ago? I reckoned Daunt knew far more about that jewellery business than he'd let on. And I don't think he liked me. When all this happened I wondered if he was trying to incriminate me in some way. I wanted to have it out with him. Then I cooled down after about a mile or so and came back. It was a hell of a night for driving in any case."

"One thing I don't understand," Hallows said. "This man who said he was Daunt. Why all the insistence on thanking you? You hadn't done anything. And how could he have had the idea—?"

"Just a minute," Cofield said. "You say the man wasn't Daunt?"

"According to the information we have, he definitely wasn't."

"Good God! You're sure?"

"I think so. So how could he have guessed that Froden would ring you straight away? Surely he'd have thought he wouldn't be seeing you till morning?"

Cofield hadn't even an idea.

"Then let's try another angle," Hallows said. "Did Daunt himself know all about the arrangements here?"

Cofield looked up.

"Daunt," he said, and licked his lips as he thought. He gave himself a little nod.

"He may have. You remember when we left Hill that morning after we'd all been talking? Well, when we came out to

Lombard Street we just walked on and then as we were passing some pub or other—"

"The Chequers?"

"That's it. Quite a nice place. Julia said she felt like a drink. She said it would do us all good, so we had a sherry. Bendale didn't come in. He had to hurry back, but we had this sherry and Daunt began asking me about myself and where I lived and so on. I believe I mentioned the Frodens." He smiled ruefully. "To tell you the truth, I don't remember what I did say."

I got up. Cofield rather stared.

"Why you talked about things being confidential when you rang me, heaven knows," I said. "Admittedly something extraordinary happened, but not to get alarmed about. In fact, as soon as I'd told you this morning about Daunt, you should have gone straight to your local police."

"But I couldn't do that?"

"Why not? It was the right thing to do. It was your duty. If the police had found out about it later, you might have been in very serious trouble. You know what you've got to do now? You and Froden have got to go back with us straightaway. Everything you've told us will have to be repeated at Scotland Yard."

You could see he hated the thought of it. Before he could speak I asked if I could use his phone.

"What're you going to do?"

"Tell Scotland Yard we're coming," I said. "They'll bring you back." I smiled. "Probably in a Rolls. If I know them, they're going to be pretty grateful."

He said he'd better tidy himself up a bit. And warn Froden. I was feeling quite pleased with myself when I got hold of Jewle. I had a very juicy plum for him which would mean maybe a few of Hallows's quids pro quo.

"We've had a bit of luck," I told him. "I can't talk any more now but we're bringing along two very important witnesses in the Daunt killing. We ought to be with you in less than an hour and a half."

I rang off before he could say a word. Ten minutes later, Cofield and Froden were ready.

After that session with Hallows and myself and the afternoon session with John Hill, Jewle was perfectly conversant with the Crewe jewellery case. As soon as I mentioned Cofield, he nodded.

"That's the late Lady Crewe's nephew? The one who's a golfer?"

It was to be a disjointed sort of hour. Jewle saw Hallows and myself in his room and Matthews was with him. We told them briefly how we'd happened to become involved with Cofield and we gave them the story as briefly as we'd heard it.

"You believed it?" Jewle asked me.

"Of course," I said. "When you see the couple, you'll know they couldn't have agreed to concoct such a yarn. Also there wasn't any earthly reason."

"You people should know," Jewle said. "How would you see them? Together or singly?"

"Since you ask—singly. Cofield chatters too much. He'd always be trying to put his spoke in. I'd see Froden first."

Hallows and I joined Cofield in the waiting-room. We made conversation but, for once, Cofield's heart wasn't in it. On the way to town he'd seemed perfectly resigned to telling his story. In that room with Hallows and me—but no Froden—he was restless again, and you could almost hear him rehearsing his story. Somehow I couldn't help wondering, as I'd wondered at Hollindale, if Froden hadn't been carefully coached, and that now the uneasiness was for the account Froden might be giving in a strange room and to people whom Cofield himself had never seen. Even at Hollindale, Cofield had been like an edgy producer of some amateur dramatic show: on tenterhooks for fear of a wrong or forgotten word and desperately ready to prompt.

In just over a quarter of an hour, Matthews brought Froden back. Cofield gave a quick, questioning look which Froden didn't really see. For him it had been something of which he'd been a bit apprehensive but which now, in retrospect, he was quite prepared to enjoy.

"A real nice gentleman, he was. Not like some o' them you see on television."

As far as we could gather, Jewle had been content to hear merely Froden's account of events. Nothing had been stressed and there'd been no puzzling questions. Another quarter of an hour passed quite quickly, then Cofield came back with Matthews. We were told the superintendent would like to see us. Cofield himself and Froden—as Jewle had told us—would be going to the morgue: Cofield to identify Daunt and Froden to be in a position to state with absolute certainty that the dead man wasn't his caller of the Sunday night.

I wanted to know how Jewle had got on with the witnesses. He told us they'd been better than most. Everything had been clear, and no discrepancies.

"You know," he said, "it's one of the most extraordinary things I ever had to listen to. You people got any explanation for it?"

I had only some glimmerings but didn't feel like suggesting them. Hallows said the whole thing was inexplicable.

"There's only one thing," he said. "Whoever it was that spoke to Froden, Daunt had to be in the car. The one that Froden later on heard leaving."

Jewle glanced at his notes. "That wasn't till ten minutes after the man left. But go on."

"What I'm getting at is this," Hallows said. "The way that car was ostensibly going, it could have gone, not to Chesham as the caller said, but to town and, if so, it could reasonably be expected to go via Harrow."

"You may be right," Jewle said. "I had roughly the same idea myself."

He had another look at his notes. "Have you people given any more thought to that theory I put up?"

I said we'd had it very much in mind.

"And don't you now agree that what happened down at Hollindale gives a certain amount of confirmation?"

What he was getting at I didn't know. I don't think Hallows did either.

"Maybe it does," I said. "How do you see things now your-self?"

"Like this," he said. "Three people are still alive who had an interest for one reason or other in that jewellery job, and two of them live within a short distance of each other. I refer to Hollindale and Newhurst. Now Daunt and the other man in the car didn't go to Hollindale to see Cofield: if they had, they'd have seen him. But they might possibly have been at Newhurst."

"Come out into the open," I said. "You mean Daunt had been seeing Mrs. Crewe at Pentlow House?"

"It could have been. If he had the diamonds, he could have been trying to drive a private bargain. Basing everything on that we'll try playing it straight. Daunt had a hired car, and his driver did get lost. It definitely was a misty night. Then Daunt picked up their whereabouts at Hollindale and sent the driver to ask about the road. Since Cofield would probably have to be disturbed, he told the driver to be sure and thank him."

"Could be," I said, and tried not to smile. "And then the driver had delusions of grandeur and said *he* was Stephen Daunt."

"It's only a theory," Jewle reminded me. "It's capable of all sorts of variations. Daunt might have been in someone's private car: the one's to whom he'd sold the diamonds, for instance. That business at Hollindale could have been as I said, and later Daunt was killed to recover the money he'd been paid. He was actually being taken back to town so that he could catch a late train for Edinburgh." He waved a hand. "It's all theories. I admit it."

"It might explain why the man said he was Stephen Daunt. Or does it?"

"It wants a lot more thinking over," Jewle told him. "But you've got to have a motive, and a starting point."

Matthews came in. Everything, he said, had been as expected. The man who'd called at Southways was definitely not the man whom Froden had seen at the morgue.

"You want to see them again, sir?"

Jewle said he didn't. When they'd signed their statements, Matthews might offer a meal and arrange for transport back. There didn't seem anything else for us either. I did ask if what had happened that evening would be given out to the Press.

"Some of it," Jewle said. "But nothing whatever to draw attention to that jewellery job. For the moment that'll be kept in the background."

"Daunt's wife ought to be back tomorrow," Hallows reminded him. "Do you think you could pass on to us where she spent the weekend?"

Jewle said he didn't see why not. He said he owed us something in any case. I've rarely known him so grateful.

I said I'd go home to the flat. Hallows said he'd walk with me the few yards to Trafalgar Square and the Tube. If Jewle had heard the opinions Hallows still had about that famous theory, our credit would not longer have been good at the Yard.

10

THE BEREAVED

HALLOWS and I started off the morning with the newspapers—half-a-dozen of them. Most had done the Daunt killing, and their readers, remarkably proud: banner headlines, exclamation marks, pictures, a lot of fact and almost as much surmise. As Hallows said, the only thing that wasn't there was Jewle's theory. There was even a reference to the Cofield-Froden business: the brief mention that Daunt was believed to have been in the neighbourhood of Hollindale at about ten-thirty on the Sunday night.

The probable time of death was given as eleven o'clock, give or take half an hour. How that death time had been reduced to within just sixty minutes, we didn't know. Perhaps Jewle had been throwing out feelers or there might be some governing medical factor of which we were unaware. But if Hallows was right in assuming that Daunt had been in the waiting car at half-past ten, and a car that, according to Froden, had left ten or fifteen minutes later, that narrowed the time of killing down to fifteen or twenty minutes.

It surely meant, too, that the car had been stopped on one pretext or other and Daunt killed within twenty minutes of leaving Hollindale. We knew that country well. There were stretches that could even be called lonely. The golf course ran along the first mile and a half of it. Somewhere there would have been the ideal spot to dump the body. Why take it on as far as Harrow?

We'd nothing else to do that morning but argue, and the more we read in the speculations of crime reporters, the more questions popped up to befog the case. That the Daunt killing was connected with the jewellery affair had to be taken for granted. John Hill had thought so, and for us that was what mattered. But what about the manner of the killing? Had it been deliberate? Or accidental? To kill a man by deliberately striking him on the temple was almost ridiculously impossible. Admittedly it had been night, and a misty one at that. Maybe then the blow had been meant for the skull generally: a blow to knock him out.

I was just thinking about coffee when Jewle rang.

"Nothing yet from Daunt's wife," he said. "If I remember rightly, you've never met her."

"But I have," I said. "It was Bob Hallows who'd never met her. You asked him, if you remember. You didn't ask me."

"You're right. Mind telling me when you saw her?"

"Less than a week ago. I wanted to have a good look at her, so I made an excuse to see Daunt about the jewellery business."

"That's fine," he said. "I hope to see her myself this morning, and I'd like to have a few ideas. What do you know about her?"

"Now you're asking," I told him. "I know quite a bit and guess at a whole lot more. It's a long story."

He thought for a moment.

"Look," he said: "I know you're probably busy but could you come along for a few minutes? I think it's important."

I treated my ego to just a second or two of hesitation and said I'd be glad to help. I'd get along straight away. As Hallows said, it was a bit of luck: not the call on Jewle but the chance that Jewle might think it necessary to take me with him when he went to Valery House.

I had to think fast during that shortish journey to the Yard. There had to be a decision what to tell and what not to tell. If I told everything, nothing would be left in reserve. If I told too little—left out, shall we say, the piquant parts—then Jewle mightn't be sufficiently interested. Even by the time I was going up to Jewle's room, I hadn't got it all sorted out. And then, even if everything had been put through the sieve, I'd have made a hash of things. One thing kept leading up to another till at last I'd told him practically all I knew. I kept back only one thing—those last few words between Templett and Caroline Daunt in Regent Street.

"A bit of luck, asking you to come along," Jewle told me. He was almost rubbing his hands. "So she was double-timing Daunt. If she wasn't, she'd have admitted you might have seen her in Regent Street. And she and Daunt weren't on the best of terms."

"As I told you, she almost certainly had an affair with Templett after that job he did for Tom Jordan on her divorce. Shortly afterwards Templett went to America and she may have married Daunt on the rebound. She was younger by best part of twenty years than he was, but she was getting on. John Parwell may have swayed her mind too. She was his step-daughter and Daunt was his nephew. It sort of kept things in the family. Financially it wasn't a bad thing for her either."

The buzzer went. Jewle's face lighted as he listened. "Right," he said. "I'll be along in about fifteen minutes."

"She's just arrived," he told me. "You think we could carry on this talk on the way there?"

There were quite a few reporters and photographers outside the entrance. Jewle waved them aside and we went through. A couple of his men were just inside and a man whom I took for the superintendent wasn't far away. Jewle asked me to wait at the foot of the stairs by the lift.

In a couple of minutes he joined me.

"Those reporters may have scared her a bit," he said. "So I had to tell her who I was and get her to see me. No hurry for a minute. She'll want time to powder her nose."

We discussed strategy: both to offer condolences then he to do the talking. There also had to be a reason for my being there. We hoped it would all fit in.

He pushed the bell and it was she who opened the door. Only a little way.

"It's all right, Mrs. Daunt. I'm Superintendent Jewle. This is Mr. Travers, who's here for business reasons. I think you've already met."

She gave a wan smile as she let us in. Her cheeks were pale and the dark beneath her eyes was definitely not mascara.

"It's all been so terrible," she said. "The shock of seeing it in the paper. I couldn't make it out. I still can't believe it."

"I'm deeply sorry," I told her. "I can't believe it either. I liked your husband enormously."

"Yes," she said. "He was a wonderful man. Whoever could have done it? He didn't have an enemy. He couldn't have had."

Jewle got her seated. We took the chesterfield.

"A terrible thing, as you say. And you'd only been married a comparatively short time. A very happy marriage too, I gather."

The sad smile came again. "It couldn't have been happier. We never knew what it was to have an angry word. I know people say that, but in our case it was true."

"Then you'll be glad to help us find those responsible."

"I will." There was a touch of vehemence. "I'll do everything I can."

"Just what I hoped for. But I shan't keep you long. Just a few necessary questions. What you thought your husband's movements would be over the weekend, for instance. He definitely told you he was going to Edinburgh?"

"He did. I'd already arranged to leave on the Saturday afternoon to spend the weekend with a friend. A very old friend, and I'd only done it because he'd told me earlier he was going to Edinburgh. He should have been leaving on the Sunday morning. It was all arranged."

"Yes," Jewle said, and a trifle heavily. "He did leave but he never got to Edinburgh. His body, as you probably read, was found at Harrow. I take it you've no idea whatever why he should have gone there." She shook her head. The tears were coming. She turned her head away as she dabbed at her eyes. We waited.

"I'm sorry," she told us. "I just couldn't help it."

"No hurry," Jewle told her soothingly. "Take your time. We're sorry to distress you like this."

She smiled bravely. "I'm all right now. I won't give way again."

"Then about your own movements during the weekend. You do understand that this is purely official." He smiled. "It's what we call just for the records."

"But of course," she said. "I got to Berkhamsted at about four and my friend met me there with her car. She lives about five miles away at Ludwold. I don't know if you've read any of her books but she's an authoress. Helen Vaile."

Jewle made a note of it "Just what we wanted to know." His forehead suddenly wrinkled. He looked round at me. "Why shouldn't we save both Mrs. Daunt and Mrs. Vaile—"

"it's Miss Vaile."

Jewle smiled. "Mrs. Daunt and *Miss* Vaile any further bother. I could ring Miss Vaile now and get it over. She's on the telephone?"

"Oh. yes. It's an easy number to remember—Ludwold 123."

The telephone was on a reproduction Sheraton table across the room. Jewle would speak quietly but I thought it as well if nothing was heard. I spoke quietly too.

"I expect you're wondering why I'm here, Mrs. Daunt. You remember I called one evening last week to see your husband."

"I remember. As soon as I saw you this morning I knew we'd met somewhere before."

I could have told her that that was rather flattering. My length, leanness, horn-rims and what have you, make me something that once seen is rarely forgotten.

"I really came to see your husband about the robbery of that jewellery."

"Jewellery?"

"You didn't know about it? He never discussed business with you?"

"Never," she told me emphatically. "Of course I'd ask him if he'd had a good day. That sort of thing, but nothing else." She smiled. "I may be old-fashioned, but I think the wife's place is the home."

Jewle was coming back.

"Well, that's over with. Miss Vaile told me everything I had to know. I don't think I'll have to trouble either of you again. In fact, I'm sure I won't."

"I was just talking to Mrs. Daunt about that jewellery business," I told him. "She was telling me her husband never brought his business home with him."

"If it was anything very special, he might have," she said. "What jewellery business was it?"

I gave her a deftly edited version. She shook her head. It was the first she'd heard about it.

"Well, at least it saved you some questions. I might have had the extremely distasteful job of asking you whether or not your husband left this flat during the weekend."

She frowned. "What weekend?"

I told her. And that, if necessary, she'd tell us he'd never left the flat.

"Saturday," she said and nodded. "Sunday."

Her lips moved as if she were going over that day's events and then she suddenly looked up.

"But he did go out. It was on the Sunday evening. He suddenly remembered he had to see somebody."

"He didn't say whom?"

"No. He just said it was somebody. I think I thought it was one of his clients."

"And how long was he away?"

She bit her lip. "Let me think. He got back about half-past seven. That's right. I remember we had a meal brought up. That makes it about—well, about an hour and a half."

"Do you remember if he took anything with him?"

She frowned in thought again. "I don't know. I remember I was reading a book and he suddenly jumped up as if he'd remembered something. I don't think I actually saw him go out."

"And did he tell you anything when he came back?"

"I don't think he did. I think he did say something about dining up here, then he went straight to the bedroom."

"I see. And please don't think I'm being in any way personal, but did you occupy separate bedrooms? It's rather fashionable these days."

"We did," she said. "But only because I'm a very bad sleeper. He hated being disturbed."

Jewle got to his feet again and held out his hand. "You've been most helpful. We're sorry to have had to intrude on you at such a time."

"You had to do it," she told him. "All I'm sorry is that I couldn't tell you more."

Tears looked not far off again. We found our own way to the door.

The car moved off. Jewle had had a word with the superintendent but he'd caught me up just outside the entrance. The little patient group closed in on us again but the car had been parked too near.

"Gone one," he told me. "I don't know about you, but I'd like a square meal."

In our job it's always good policy to eat when you can. An hour often cometh when you'd love to eat but the pangs have to go on gnawing.

"Might as well try our usual place," he said. "I'm in the chair, by the way. The least I owe you is a lunch."

He asked me what I thought of things generally. I said she'd done an awful lot of highly artistic lying.

"And the tears?"

I smiled. "Women aren't like men. You know Bernice well enough. She's a very intelligent woman, but sometimes she mentions an old aunt of hers of whom she was very fond. She says, 'Poor Aunt Evelyn', and if I didn't head her off with some remark or other, she'd be dabbing at her eyes."

"I know," he said. "I'm married too. All Mrs. Daunt had to do was conjure up something and out the tears'd come. Even if you hadn't put me wise before we got there, I'd have said she was lying. I'm having a record kept of her telephone calls from the flat, by the way."

It's quite a short drive, and as we neared Trafalgar Square I thought of asking him to have the car stopped just in Northumberland Avenue. Then I changed my mind. What I'd thought of doing was something which it might be as well to keep to myself. All I did remind him of before the car actually drew up, was that Caroline Daunt had been a model. And a model, if she's anywhere near the top grade, has to be something of an actress. Maybe it was one of my more high-falutin remarks. All Jewle did was nod.

We were in that restaurant about half an hour and all the time we talked. Two things only might interest you. One was when Jewle suddenly reached for the menu, felt for a pencil and began drawing a rough map on the back.

"This is what I can't get away from. Everything to do with the Daunt case and the jewellery took place in this comparatively small area. The Crewes are at Pentlow House, Newhurst; Cofield at Hollindale and Daunt's body was found at Harrow. You can almost spit from one place to another. And Mrs. Daunt was spending the weekend near Berkhamsted. There must be more in it than we've seen."

If there was, we couldn't find it. I'd called attention to the very same thing myself.

"There's something else," he said. "I don't know if I told you, but Cofield's man Froden didn't spend the weekend at Hollindale. He and his wife, so he told me, occasionally have a Sunday off to go to Newhurst. Both born and bred there. Relations still living there, and that's where they were on Sunday. Froden made no bones about telling me the whole thing. He and his wife generally pack up for the night after Cofield's evening meal, and that's usually at seven. Cofield had told them a day or two beforehand about having the Sunday off, so they took a local bus at nine o'clock on the Sunday morning. They didn't see Cofield because he said he'd be lying in late. He generally did. Then on the Sunday night they got back about nine. They didn't see Cofield and he'd ring if he wanted anything, which he didn't. In other words, they'd only been home about an hour before that caller arrived. Froden had only just turned out the light."

If he was making a point he didn't labour it. The other thing he mentioned was what Caroline Daunt had told us about her husband's leaving the flat on the night of November the third.

"You ought to be feeling pretty pleased about that," he told me. "It looks as if you've broken the back of that jewellery job."

"You think that for some special reason of his own, Daunt went to Saffron Row and substituted the replicas?"

He looked surprised at the question. "Well, didn't he?"

"He could have," I said, and smiled a bit wryly. "But if that's your idea of a case being over, I only wish it were mine. Besides, there's something else. She might have been lying about the whole thing. We know she was lying about pretty nearly everything else, so why not that?"

Naturally I didn't tell him so, but he was still fitting things into that theory of his. It was an *idée fixe* that Daunt had been in possession of the diamonds. His whole theory was based on it. Jewle rarely purrs with satisfaction, but he'd been a long way from disappointed about that evening absence of Daunt from his flat.

When we came out we stood for a moment at the parting of the ways. "Are you people going to interview that Helen Vaile?" I asked him.

"We might have to sooner or later. Why?"

"I'd like to see her myself, say in the morning. I can't get away from the idea that I've run across her name somewhere recently, and not in connection with books."

"Don't see why you shouldn't," he said. "You might let me know how you get on."

He'd offered to have a car take me back to Broad Street, but I'd said I'd like to stretch my legs at least as far as Duncannon Street and a bus. What I had in mind was a bookshop just short of the Strand. A middle-aged assistant came towards me from the back of the shop.

"Do you happen to have anything by a Helen Vaile?"

"Helen Vaile," he said. "No, sir. I'm afraid we don't, but we could get it for you."

"What sort of things does she write?"

"Romances, sir. Love stories. They're usually quite popular."

"You mean that hers aren't?"

He smiled. "I didn't say that, sir. I admit we don't often get asked for them."

He looked up a catalogue and gave me the name of what seemed her last—*Hearts Entwined*.

"You could get me a copy by the morning?"

He said he could. I gave him my card and said I'd drop in at about nine.

Hallows' eyes popped when I told him about Helen Vaile. As far as Caroline Daunt was concerned she was indeed a very old friend. One might say a friend in need. She'd been the one who'd given evidence when Caroline had secured her decree against her husband.

"Maybe that alibi isn't worth a hoot," he said. "No one could claim it as impartial."

I told him we were going to pay a call on the lady in the morning, and then the buzzer went. Jewle was on the line.

"Something rather important I learned when I got back here," he said. "A constable was cycling home on the A 40 about six miles out of Rickmansworth at about eleven o'clock on the Sunday night, when he was nearly run down by a car. He hollered and immediately the car's lights were switched off and it gathered speed. He caught a glimpse of a couple of men just as he hollered, and the driver was wearing a snap-brimmed hat. It's thought the light was turned off so the number couldn't be taken."

"You think it had Daunt's body in it?"

"I think it's highly likely. And that's why the body was dumped in a side road at the very next place—Harrow. That policeman might have sent a warning ahead as far as they knew, and the car might have been stopped."

I said it sounded very feasible. "Where *should* the body have gone, do you think?"

"To somewhere in the neighbourhood of King's Cross Station," he said. "To tie in with that supposed trip to Edinburgh. Don't you agree?"

I did agree and I told him so. Hallows agreed, too. He did add a private rider to the effect that it was amazing what luck you had when you were trying to bolster up a dud theory.

"Haven't you got your own private bee in your bonnet?" I asked him. "What's the real flaw in his theory?"

He looked surprised. "Daunt, of course. I'll bet everything I have that he could never have indulged in anything shady. There's no shred of real evidence to the contrary, in spite of what the lady told you and Jewle. You'd like to have a small bet yourself?"

I took the coward's way out. Said he was probably right. The last twice we'd had a bet, I'd had to pay out.

11

FIND THE LADY

I DIDN'T go to the office that morning. Hallows was meeting me at the flat at nine-thirty and then we'd start off for Berkhamsted. At nine o'clock, of course, I had to pick up *Hearts Entwined*.

It was waiting for me. The jacket, which might have been a still from one of the slightly less nauseating television ads., showed two smiling young people cheek to cheek and with arms round each other's shoulders. Behind them was a tropical beach with coconut palms and a very blue sea. The lettering beneath the author's name said she had also written *Trick of Fate*. I ought perhaps to have recognised the name of the publisher, but I didn't. I opened the book at a chance page and read a few lines. It was far from badly written.

Perhaps what I've said reveals a certain intellectual arrogance. I hope not. Let me tell you a story: a true story. When I was young and just down from Cambridge I wrote a couple of books which, unfortunately, were extremely well reviewed. I didn't give myself any public airs, but deep inside me was the knowledge that I was possessed of almost all the literary virtues. I imagine that you, too, can wince today at the callowness of your youth.

Then one day I was calling at my agents. The partner who handled me was a superbly competent woman who'd come up via Fleet Street and was no great respecter of persons, even someone like myself. Several books were on her desk and I happened to pick one up. It was a love romance. I laid it down with a smile.

"Do you know how much we paid the writer of that book in royalties last year?" I was asked. "Over three thousand pounds. She's probably the one who's having a quiet laugh at *you*."

I don't say that neat verbal dressing-down was followed by a miraculous cure, but at least it made me think. My two books, even over the years, didn't bring me anything like three thousand pounds. I just hadn't the readers. Mind you, as I looked at *Hearts Entwined*, I doubted if Helen Vaile had the readers either.

I looked at the picture on the back of the jacket and for a moment I couldn't believe my eyes. What I was looking at was incredible. I read the letter-press beneath. It said that Helen Vaile had spent her early years in France but later had been educated in England. She was rapidly becoming recognised as one of the most delightful and enthralling writers of romantic fiction. There probably wasn't a magazine that hadn't at some time or other printed one of her short stories.

When I went down to fetch the car I slipped the book into my overcoat pocket. I didn't want Hallows to see it—as yet. As a matter of fact we didn't talk about the case at all till we were nearing Berkhamsted and watching for a signpost. The village of Ludwold was about five miles to the west, and it was getting on for eleven o'clock by the time we reached it. It was larger that we'd thought. The house, we were told, was called Windover, and it took quite a bit of finding: we finally ran it to earth at the beginning of a line of fairly new bungalows in a side lane. It was a brick-built, two-storey cottage with a wooden garage at the side. Its small front garden was far from tidy, and the woodwork was definitely in need of paint. It didn't look as if Helen Vaile was in the three thousand a year class. But she did have television and the telephone was connected.

I'd luckily stopped the car a few yards short of the house. That was when I gave Hallows the book.

"You'd better take a look at this," I said, "otherwise you might get a shock when we go into the house."

He looked at the front, then at the back.

"Good heavens!" he said, "It can't be."

"It is," I said. "All the same, there's no need to change a thing. Just do everything as planned."

I pushed the bell. There was a movement of the curtain at the window on my right. A second or two and the door was opened. The look was quizzical but pleasant.

"Yes?"

That picture on the back of the jacket hadn't done her justice. The face had far more character. She wasn't good-looking but she was a long way from unattractive. She was shortish and plump, but the plumpness gave her face at least an amiability.

I flashed the agency card at her.

"Miss Vaile?"

"Yes," she said, and waited.

"My name's Travers and this is my colleague, Mr. Hallows. I was in Mrs. Daunt's apartment yesterday morning when Superintendent Jewle rang you."

She didn't let me finish. "Of course. Do come in."

She had a pleasant if somewhat throaty voice. She carried herself well as she walked.

"How was Mrs. Daunt? I almost went with her myself but she wouldn't let me. A tremendous shock, you know, suddenly reading news like that. They were such a devoted couple."

I'd been running my eye round the room: a cottage parlour that had been turned into a workroom-lounge. A flat-topped desk had been placed with its back slightly askew to one of the windows, and on it was a typewriter and a pile of manuscript paper. There were just two easy chairs and the television set was a seventeen-inch. A rather dull fire was burning in the

Victorian grate. The room had the faint haziness of cigarette smoke, and there was also a faint touch of perfume.

I assured her that Mrs. Daunt, when I'd left her, had seemed far less distressed. "She hasn't rung you?"

"No," she said. "I was expecting her to ring this morning." We'd come prepared with a sheet of official paper on which various things were typed. I explained. Confirmation of Mrs. Daunt's whereabouts had been only verbal and we'd merely come to have everything official. She had a look at the paper.

"And what am I to say?"

It may have been artless by design. I suggested certain words and she repeated them. She asked if she could type them and then write from the copy. I told her it was an excellent suggestion. What was finally arrived at was this:

This is a statement by me, Helen Vaile, spinster of Windover, Ludwold, Bucks., relative to the whereabouts of Caroline Daunt, now a widow, of apartment seventeen, Valery House, South Kensington, from Saturday the ninth of November, 1963 to Tuesday the twelfth of November in the same year . . .

She signed at the foot. Hallows, as witness, signed in the space provided.

"You see?" I said, as I put the paper in its envelope. "Nothing formidable at all."

"It was just that I'd never done anything of the sort before. But won't you sit down. And do let me make you some coffee. Perhaps one of you would stir up the fire."

Coffee, I said, was an excellent idea. After all, if she wanted to talk we were only too ready to oblige. Hallows saw to the fire. I placed the easy chairs and brought in a small side-table. The kettle must have been on the boil, for coffee came in almost at once. There was also a plate of biscuits on the tray.

"I hope you don't mind instant coffee? I'm afraid I haven't any cream."

I said it looked to me like positive luxury. She swivelled the desk chair round towards the fire, and in less than no time we were chatting away like old friends. Maybe I should confine the talk to a few of her actual statements. The rest was largely amiable but irrelevant chatter . . .

"Of course you don't really know her but she's an absolute dear. We've been friends for years. We were at school together, you know. I didn't know Stephen, of course, till they were married. To tell you the truth I was just a bit worried about it at the time, but how wrong I was! It was an absolutely perfect marriage. He was always so reliable."

"Oh, I get by. Television, of course, has practically ruined books. Do you know that where the libraries used to take blocks of a hundred and fifty or two hundred, now it's only about fifty? All those little libraries are out of business too. I'm really lucky, you know, to do as well as I do."

"There wasn't a single bungalow anywhere near when I bought the cottage seven years ago. Now they've utterly ruined everything. It used to be such a lovely little lane. That's why I'm selling the cottage as soon as I get back from my holiday. I think I'll find somewhere nearer town."

"Oh, in France: a little village near Nimes. I was brought up there as a girl, you know. But not before another week. I really must get that manuscript away to my publishers. I'm rather finicky about everything being just as it should be."

We started back the way we'd come. At the four-cross ways was a signpost. We took the little road that said: to Penfield and Newhurst. A little way along I drew the car up. "You're satisfied she's the one?"

Hallows said there was no doubt about it.

"Got any ideas?"

"Well, there's something very fishy about Caroline Daunt's alibi. That's certain. Don't ask me if she had anything to do with killing her husband. I doubt if she did."

Unless the Daunts had put up a show when Helen Vaile was present, she was also a fluent liar. I doubted if two such close friends would obscure the truth.

I moved the car on and we kept the other questions in the background. It would be different when we had positive proof, which shouldn't be difficult at Pentlow House. It was after midday, however, and we didn't want to put the Crewes to the dilemma of lunch, so we pulled up at the Newhurst pub and had a lunch of sorts there. We spun things out, and it was nearing two o'clock when we moved on.

Robert opened the door. He seemed quite pleased to see us. Both the Crewes were in. The master had just woke up after his nap, and Robert had just taken *The Times* to the study.

"Perhaps Mr. Crewe will see us there," I said. "Will you ask him? We'd like you to be there, too."

A couple of minutes and he was showing us in. Crewe, too, seemed pleased to see us. He asked if we'd had lunch. Would we at least have coffee. I said we were rather pressed for time. What we'd come about was the identification of the woman who'd called the day before he'd arrived from Kenya. She'd said she was a journalist who'd been commissioned to write an article on the late Lady Crewe.

"I remember," he said. "Robert saw her and then she saw Alan. He managed to get her to leave. It was all in very bad taste."

"Is that the woman?"

Robert had a look at the picture on the jacket. He looked at me. He looked at the picture again.

"That's her, sir."

"You're absolutely sure?"

"Yes, sir. Absolutely sure."

"You'd swear to it in a court of Law?"

He moistened his lips. "Yes, sir, if I had to."

I thanked him and told him that'd be all. Crewe was looking puzzled.

"A court of law?" he said. "You mean the woman was some sort of criminal?"

"We're not sure," I said. "What we do know is that she came here on wholly false pretences. No women's magazine, no commission."

"Then what *did* she come for?"

I said we didn't know. We had ideas and we'd follow them up. One thing was certain. She was involved in some way in the matter of the jewellery substitution.

"What we've told you is highly confidential. All we hope is it'll lead to the whole of that jewellery business being sorted out."

He said he devoutly hoped so. Might he give the news to his wife? I saw no reason why he shouldn't.

"That terrible business about Daunt," he said. "We've been afraid to ask any questions, but do you think that was all part of the same thing?"

I didn't commit myself. Everything had gone out of our hands, was what I said—including John Hill's. Scotland Yard had taken over the case. We were merely co-operating when called upon.

"It's all a tragedy," he said. "Everybody wanted to avoid publicity, and now this has happened. We could have been quietly enjoying our stay here just for these few weeks, but it's always somewhere in the background."

Julia Crewe came in. She seemed her imperturbable self. The news had to be given all over again. She gave her husband a look.

"Do you think I should mention this morning?"

"Yes," he said. "I think you should. It's about Alan," he told us. "But you tell them, my dear."

"He came here this morning," she said. "I thought it was one of his usual visits, and then he said he wanted to speak to me privately. He said he was in some sort of trouble and wanted me to lend him quite a large sum of money. All I could do was refer him to David."

"He gave you no idea what the money was for?"

"I gathered it was to settle a debt of some sort. I really do think it was genuine. He was looking so shockingly ill. Didn't you think so, David?"

"Either ill or suffering from a bad hangover. I wouldn't like you gentlemen to get the impression that Alan's a bone of contention between me and Mrs. Crewe. It's just understood between us that I haven't any particular use for him. What I'm trying to convey is that Alan knew very well how I felt, so when he came to me he was doing something extremely distasteful."

"He was in big trouble," I said. "You feel like telling us how much money he wanted?"

"Fifteen hundred pounds. When I said it was absolutely impossible, he reduced it to a thousand. He said he'd sign any kind of note guaranteeing repayment against what my mother left him."

"A lot of money," I said. "You didn't lend it?"

"No," he said. "What I did say was that I'd consider the matter on the condition that he'd give me every detail about why the money was wanted. I gave him to understand that I'd make my own enquiries before advancing the money." He allowed himself a smile. "I hope I wasn't being pious."

"And he said?"

"He said he'd have to think things over too." He gave his wife a quick look. "I think we must ask Mr. Travers to regard what we've been telling him as confidential. I think we can deal with Alan ourselves."

"You're quite right to wish to keep it to yourselves," Hallows told him. "It's a family matter. Perhaps you'll be so good, though, as to tell us just as confidentially of any developments."

Julia Crewe said they'd be only too happy to do so, and that just about concluded the call. We said goodbye to David Crewe but she went out with us to the car. It was one of those rare November afternoons when the sky is clear, the trees have more colours than even Shelley's autumn leaves, and you find yourself taking deep breaths of air. Julia Crewe stood for a moment on the bottom step and looked across the valley.

"Thinking of Kenya?" I asked her quietly.

"Yes," she said. And then, almost fiercely: "God knows what I wouldn't give to be back there."

I'd have liked to use the Crewe telephone to ring Jewle but had thought better of it. What I did was drop in at the police station at Rickmansworth. He wasn't in, but Matthews said he ought to be back by the time I arrived. Hallows dropped me at the Yard and drove the car back to the garage. I wouldn't be seeing him again till the morning.

Jewle was in. He'd not long arrived and was having a cup of tea. He sent down for one for me too.

"You've been seeing Miss Vaile?" he said.

I gave him the signed and witnessed statement. I admitted we'd rather jumped the gun, but we'd had to have some excuse for the call.

He had a look at it. He was smiling wryly as he passed it to Matthews.

"Quite a professional job. I wonder sometimes what you people'd do if you decided to take to crime." He waved the hand of dismissal. "How'd you get on with her otherwise?"

"Hallows was with me, and in our considered opinion there's something very suspicious about the alibi of Caroline Daunt's."

"Any why? Something additional to what we thought when we saw her?"

I said the two stories fitted in too snugly : a kind of course of bricks with fake cement. Both women had begun by trying to convince us that the Daunt marriage had been made in heaven and lived in Eden. Hallows and I were sure that both statements had been agreed on soon after Caroline Daunt had read of her husband's death.

"You don't think they had a hand in it?" Matthews said.

"From what we know so far, I don't see how either of them could. What I'm more and more convinced of, though, is that they know a whole lot we'd like to know. You don't bolster up a genuine alibi with lies."

Jewle wanted to know about the Vaile woman herself. I showed him the picture on the back of the jacket, and I was wondering if I could avoid telling him about her call at Pentlow House. I didn't want the Crewes pestered, and yet I ought to make a clean breast. What I decided on was a compromise.

Matthews was looking at the picture.

"A bit dowdy," he said. "How well do you think she was off financially?"

I described the cottage and told him what she'd said about the sales of her books. He gave me an opening when he said that even if she'd had no hand whatever in the Daunt killing, she might know quite a lot about the jewellery business.

"I was coming to that," I said to Jewle. "You remember I told you yesterday I was sure I'd seen Helen Vaile somewhere before? That was after I'd bought that book and seen her photograph. It turned out that I'd never actually seen her, neither had Hallows, but he'd remembered a story the butler at Pentlow House had told him along with the woman's description and Hallows had reported it to me."

I told him the whole story. It seemed to fascinate him. His eyes never left my face.

"But why?" he said. "Where're the connections? How does it tie in?"

I thought I knew, but I wasn't going to tell him. I just shrugged my shoulders.

"You people could ask her. If you do, I doubt whether she'll deny it. She'll almost certainly say she was acting as a free lance and that talk of a commission was just an excuse."

"There has to be something in it," Jewle said doggedly. "She had a talk with Cofield, you said?"

"Yes, and Cofield lied about it. He later told the Crewes he'd sent her away almost at once with a flea in her ear. Robert, the butler, says the two were talking for best part of half an hour. And almost certainly not about Lady Crewe. Remember, we've not been able to trace any article on Lady Crewe. By the way, I don't think you'll catch the Vaile woman out over that. She'll probably say she realised after all there wasn't a story in it."

"Women!" Matthews said. "I'd rather deal with fifty men than a couple of women."

I told them there was something else they ought to know. Take the facts we now had. Vaile had met Cofield. Cofield was at least a suspect in the jewellery affair. Vaile and Caroline Daunt were friends and allies. Caroline Daunt had tried to throw suspicion on her husband with that tale of a Sunday night absence from the apartment.

"Admit it's some of it conjecture," I said, "but surely it adds up to something. Have a wild guess and say the three people mentioned know at least the whereabouts of the stolen diamonds. If so, what about this?"

I told them how Helen Vaile had carefully led the talk that morning to selling her cottage as soon as she returned from a holiday in France—the France where she'd been brought up as a girl. It was almost certain that she spoke the language fluently.

"She talked of leaving in about a week. Could it be a week because she wants all the dust to settle? Is she the courier who's taking the diamonds for disposal in France?"

Jewle clicked his tongue exasperatedly. "Too much to digest on the spur of the moment. It's shoving a crossword under our noses and expecting us to write the clues straight away down."

"I know," I said. "Mind if I say one other thing?"

He waved a hand.

"It's this: God forbid I should tell you your business, but were I you, I'd have that Vaile woman under close observation from now on. What about telephone calls, by the way?"

He said he'd actually been with the superintendent at Valery House when I'd rung. There'd been no calls whatever. At about two o'clock, however, Mrs. Daunt had rung down to ask if all the reporters had gone. He told her they had. A few minutes later she went out. It looked as if she was taking care not to have any calls traced.

He said he'd also learned quite a few things about Daunt. He and the superintendent had appeared to have quite a liking for each other and often had quite a chat when they happened to meet. Valery House had a licence only for drinks consumed in its restaurant but Gill—the superintendent—sometimes obliged Daunt with a bottle of whiskey when he happened suddenly to run short. Irish whiskey. Daunt always had a hot toddy in bed during the cold months, and he'd sip it while he wrote his private diary.

12

OUT OF THE PAST

I GOT to the office rather earlier the next morning, and among my correspondence was a letter from the McGuffie Agency in

New York. I'd almost forgotten that I'd asked for information about Templett.

It was an air-mail letter and, before I'd read half of it, I knew it was one of the strangest letters I'd ever received. Even though I knew McGuffie. You might say I took him over with my own agency when I acquired it, and that's more years ago than I like remembering.

Dear Travers,

I'm sorry to have been so long over the assignment and not to be in a position even now to give you the information required.

As you know, we're far from a closed circle here, so we did have a little difficulty in tracing the subject. You didn't furnish us with exact dates but it seems that not long after his arrival here he secured employment as an operative with what I must call A-Investigations: hereafter A-I. Fifteen months later he left them. Every likely source was cagey about the exact reason for his leaving. My own guess is that it was a dismissal. This is why.

Some three months later he joined B-Investigations. Shortly before he returned to England there were rumours of a scandal concerning B-I, and its licence to operate was withdrawn. Since the owner was an ex-police captain of the highest reputation, the feeling was that he'd been some sort of scapegoat. Remember that we had to dig back to some years ago and it's as good as impossible to find witnesses. I do have it, however, on reasonably good authority that the subject and another operative were sacked. The same authority claims that the owner of B-I was heard to tell the subject that if ever he as much as saw him again, he'd shoot him.

Even using the rumours mentioned, I was unable to obtain further information from A-I. I see little hope of discovering anything further. I would add that in at least the case of B-I, rumour has it that certain influential parties concerned brought pressure to cover up what could have been a major scandal.

You gave no definite reasons for the assignment, but if you wanted him enquired into before employing him yourself, I do advise you strongly not to do so. I hope to be in London in a few days' time and shall look forward to seeing you. We could perhaps talk a bit more freely then.

Sincerely,

B. McGuffie.

An extraordinary letter. It told so much and so tantalisingly little. I'd just read it a second time when Hallows arrived. I showed it to him.

"If you remember, I never actually met Templett," he said. "We were going to reopen the case he'd been handling when something happened to stop it."

"That's right," I said. "We were working for a woman named Eva Strand and she committed suicide. But McGuffie's letter. What's your impression?"

He said he didn't quite know what to make of it. If anything could be read into it, it was that Templett had been sacked from two jobs in New York, and probably on each occasion for something distinctly fishy. What was I going to do about it?

I went to Norris's room and came back with the Strand file. Together we went over every detail of what had happened. Hallows was disinclined to express an opinion. If he were forced, he said, he'd say that Eva Strand had been mentally unbalanced from the very start. Templett had unearthed nothing but gaps and discrepancies. He'd probably been looking for a Ruth Rawson who'd never existed.

I said we'd shift to something else: something that made Templett quite a difference person.

"He came back here about a year ago and with enough funds to operate his own agency. You can't exactly do that on peanuts, not that I'm interested in where he got the money from. It could have been legitimate, and even if it wasn't we can't do anything about it. What interests me is how he suddenly popped up from nowhere in connection with Caroline Daunt? Remember what he told her at the end of that meeting in Regent Street? 'You're going to be damn sorry about this—you and your boy-friend.'"

Hallows did some thinking. "He'd had an affair with her and he tried to renew it when he got back, and she wasn't having any."

He did some more thinking. "Looks as if he'd been having her followed. He wouldn't have mentioned a boyfriend if there wasn't any truth in it."

"My idea too," I told him. "Coincidences are tricky things. They can be natural and they can be manufactured. Templett warned her she was going to be sorry, and sorry she is. The devil of a lot of things have happened to her since that meeting in Regent Street."

"Yes," he said. "But again it may have been only a coincidence."

"I know," I said. "But something keeps telling me it isn't. Assume, for instance, that Templett did have her watched and followed. Couldn't that have put him in possession of something of importance in the jewellery case?"

He smiled.

"But no one knew about the jewellery case. It was all being kept nice and snug in the family."

He was right. There'd been something far from impeccable about my logic. I tried to do some thinking along different lines but it wasn't any good.

"Look," he said. "We're at a loose end for the moment. If your hunch is all that strong, why not put in a little time on

Templett. What was your opinion of his handling of that Strand case, for example?"

I said I'd had no reason whatever to complain. All the same, there'd been various curious things about it. I told him about that maudlin speech Templett had made when we'd said goodbye, and then he remembered something himself: that extraordinary outburst by Mrs. Strand when I'd rung her up to report progress.

I picked up the Strand file and got to my feet.

"Right," I said. "We look like having a day on our hands, so we'll re-open the Strand case. It'll be a cold scent but you never know."

"Good," he said. "Where do we start?"

"Where Templett did," I told him. "At Somerset House."

I asked first for a certified copy of the marriage certificate of a Will or William Rawson to a Janice—maiden name unknown. The marriage might have taken place in 1942, and in Norfolk. I was looking rather like a lawyer with that brief-case containing the Strand file, and the man attending to me just nodded understanding when I apologised for the gaps in the information.

We waited and waited. It was quite twenty minutes before he reappeared.

"We have a certificate corresponding in some ways to the one you require," he told me, "but the date doesn't agree. This particular marriage took place in 1927."

"The names agree?"

"Yes," he said. "A William Rawson to a Janice Hart. The marriage was celebrated in Norfolk, as you said. You'd like the copy?"

I took the certified copy and paid the fee. We moved a little distance away and had a good look at it. What it told us was that on the 19th of April, 1927, a William Richard Rawson, aged

26, a farmer residing at Hemwell in the county of Norfolk, had been united in holy matrimony at the parish church, Hemwell, with a Janice Elizabeth Hart, also residing at Hemwell. Her father was a medical practitioner and his a farmer.

It just had to be the couple who'd befriended Eva Strand in or about 1943. But by then the couple had been married sixteen years, so how could they have been remembered as only a recently married couple?

"Mrs. Strand was mentally sick when she saw you," Hallows said. "Some sort of truth was there, but the facts were muddled."

"Right," I said. "Let's try a flank attack. You get a certified copy of the birth of a daughter, Ruth."

I thought back to the instructions I'd given Templett and I began asking myself questions. If he'd obtained a certified copy of the marriage certificate, it'd have been among the receipt vouchers which I'd paid when he'd left. All he'd done was inspect the brief summary of facts which can be provided as a check before the purchase of a certified copy. But why? It wasn't his own money he was spending. It was mine.

I thought back to the first report he'd made. I'd asked how he'd got on at Somerset House and he'd said that everything had been in order. That could have meant only one thing, that the facts with which I'd provided him had been as stated: that the young couple had been duly married in or about 1942 and in 1943 had had a baby daughter whom they'd named Ruth. But they hadn't been married in or about 1942. By that year they were a couple who'd been married some sixteen years and at over forty they couldn't be described as young.

What grounds, then, could Templett possibly have had for telling me that everything had been in order? The obvious difference from the facts provided must have told him at once that something was badly wrong and then the proper course of action would have been to have telephoned me or seen me before proceeding any further with the case.

But he hadn't. What he'd apparently done was to go at once to Norwich.

Hallows seemed to be a mighty long time but at last he came back.

"Can't make it out," he said. "There's no record whatever of the birth of a daughter, Ruth, to that couple."

A few yards on was a place where we could get coffee and it was there that we tried to lick some sort of sense into what we'd discovered. We tried looking at things from the angle of Eva Strand and I had to give it as my considered opinion that, mentally ill or not, she had showed no special signs of it in my office. Nervous, yes, but most people are when for the first time they find it necessary to visit a detective agency. Ill, maybe yes, but not in the accepted sense. The tragic death of her only daughter had brought on a mental sickness from which she was recovering. My opinion was that she had actually recovered from it mentally and that the rather tired look had been a kind of after product. In the office she'd been coherent and, considering the lapse of time, reasonably sure of her facts.

"What about that insistence on her husband not being told?"

I admitted that had puzzled me. That after the death of her own daughter she should have felt the urge to do something for the daughter of people who'd once befriended her was perfectly natural: it was the insistence on secrecy that was wrong. Surely her husband should have been only too pleased at such a befriending. The Martin Strand I knew would have done everything to help.

"The facts weren't right either," Hallows said. "What about her statement that the couple had been living in Newmarket Road?"

Something was beginning to dawn on me. If Templett had deceived me deliberately about his Somerset House checking being in order, why shouldn't the rest of his reports have contained deliberate deceptions?

"Perfectly easy to find out," Hallows said. "Let's get along to this Hemwell place and see. Even if the Rawsons have moved, there ought to be some kind of trail."

We got up at once. We picked up my car at St. Martin's and headed north for Tottenham and Ware. We stopped at Royston and had a quick lunch, and took the Newmarket Road. It was a magnificent road for travelling and there wasn't more than a sprinkle of traffic. On the open heath beyond Thetford we pulled up for another look at the map. Hemwell was some twenty miles to the north-east, and a few miles on we took a side road. The roads became much more narrow and, what with checking sign-posts, we travelled far more slowly. It was nearing three o'clock when at last we entered the village. A tractor drawing a trailer was approaching us.

"Is there a Mr. William Rawson farming about here?"

"Why, yes," the driver said. "He farm at Scotgate. You want to see him?"

I said we did.

"Then you go back to the cross-roads and turn left. It's about a mile on. You'll see a notice what say Scotgate."

We let him get well away before we made the turn. I drove on and we didn't speak. You don't feel like talking when you're on the very edge of discovery.

We saw the handsomely painted board when we were quite a way from it. We turned into a private road more even and better kept than the one we'd left. We went through a little spinney and there was the farm. I pulled the car up.

"Looks quite a big place," Hallows said. "I have an idea I'm smelling money."

The house itself looked late Georgian, smallish but snug. Behind it was quite a range of buildings. To our left men were working with tractors and trailers and a couple of sugar-beet lifters and loaders. Immediately to our right was a meadow on which were a series of jumps: the headquarters, perhaps, of a pony club or riding school. Beyond that was the dark green of winter wheat. As Hallows had said, the placed looked like money.

The iron gate that led to the semi-circular drive was open. I drew the car in at the front door. I had to push the bell a second time. A rosy-cheeked woman who looked about sixty opened the door. I lifted my hat.

"Is Mr. Rawson in?"

She smiled. "I think so, sir. I think he's in his office. If you wait here a minute, I'll see."

We didn't have long to wait. We went across a small entrance hall and along a short passage to a door on which she tapped. A voice called something. She smiled and drew back. We went in.

"Mr. Rawson?" I said. "Mr. William Rawson?"

"That's right," he said. "I don't think I know you gentlemen." He smiled. "Who is it this time? The ministry?"

He was a burly, thick-set man who just about looked his age. He'd spoken with barely a trace of accent. He was wearing riding breeches and a turtle-necked sweater, and his coat was a good quality tweed. There was something about him immediately likeable. Maybe it'd been the way he'd smiled. I smiled too and waved at the desk.

"I see they're still not sparing the forms?"

He grimaced. "Don't talk to me about forms. You're a farmer yourself?"

"No," I said, "but I read the newspapers. And my father used to farm not a hundred miles from here. I'm East Anglian born and bred."

"You are?" The smile came again. "D'yer father keep a dicky, bor?"

I couldn't help smiling as he fired that ancient Norfolk shibboleth at me: the one that's been used for ages to find out if a man's what he claims. In case you don't know, it asks if your father keeps a donkey. Spoken quickly it sounds like gibberish.

"He do," I told him. "Are you for sale then?"

He laughed. I'd given the orthodox answer.

"You're Norfolk all right. And now what can I do for you?"

It was ticklish work explaining. The more I talked, the more mystified he looked.

"Four years ago, and a woman named Eva Strand wanted to leave some money to my daughter, Ruth. I don't understand it. It beats me altogether. I never heard of the woman."

"But you do have a daughter, Ruth?"

"Yes," he said, and then his eyes narrowed.

"Wait a minute. I think my wife ought to hear this. I'll find her."

We heard him calling. In a couple of minutes she was coming in. She was a good-looking woman, well-dressed and well-spoken.

"Would you mind telling my wife what you told me?"

I told her, as I'd told him, that everything said in that room would be in the strictest confidence: then I went over everything again. She was looking mystified too. That was at the beginning: towards the end there was a look like the imminence of fright.

"Correct me if I'm wrong," I said, "but you people do know something about this. Why not tell us? Mr. Hallows and I are reputable. As I told your husband, Mrs. Rawson, you've only to ring New Scotland Yard to have our credentials verified. Ring them now. There's plenty of time."

They looked at each other. "You tell them," she said.

He told us. Four years ago another man had called. He, too, was making enquiries about the daughter, and he too had mentioned a legacy. He'd also known that Ruth wasn't a real daughter: that, in fact, she'd been adopted. It was something that Hallows and I had guessed at ourselves.

"And you never saw the man afterwards?"

"Never."

"A youngish man, tall and dark-haired?"

"That was him. Very pleasant mannered."

"Did he by any chance say his name was Templett?" They looked at each other again.

"That wasn't the name he gave," Rawson said. "It was Harrison. We've never forgotten it. He said he was representing some solicitors and he had to make sure we did actually have a daughter Ruth."

I told them the man had been a scoundrel. The police were looking for him and, since he'd once been employed by our firm, we were assisting. Unfortunately, Eva Strand was dead. That's why we'd come to Hemwell.

"She must have been that woman."

She'd said that to her husband.

"Tell us about it," I said. "Neither of you wants the police here making enquiries. Everything you tell us now will be kept strictly to ourselves. You have my word."

This was the story that emerged. Let me say at once that I've never had to do with an adoption case. I know no more than the average layman, and even that is somewhat vague. When it comes to what conditions were like twenty years ago, I'm a very long way from sure. But to get on with the story.

The Rawsons had despaired of having children and had decided to adopt one. Mrs. Rawson wanted a daughter. Her father, the doctor, did regular stints as an obstetrician at a maternity home near Norwich and it was he who gave them the news that there was a baby girl available. For the purposes of the legal side of the affair, the Rawsons stayed at Norwich for some days, with Mrs. Rawson's brother who was then living in Newmarket Road.

One afternoon a woman called at the house when the Rawsons themselves happened to be out and the sister-in-law spoke to her. She wanted to know if she was the one who was adopting a baby girl. The sister-in-law said it wasn't her but her husband's sister, and wanted to know what the call was about. The woman said she was representing a society that always made sure that the adopting parents were fit and proper people. She was assured they were and then she left.

"Tell Mr. Travers about the photograph."

Templett, it appeared, had had a photograph and he wanted to know if it was of the woman who'd called at the house in Newmarket Road. The Rawsons said they'd find out and ring him at the Norwich Hotel. Rawson and his wife went straight to Norwich where the photograph was verified as being the woman who'd called. Templett was notified and that was the last they'd heard of him.

I said I couldn't understand it. "Surely everything connected with an adoption was kept absolutely secret? How could the woman possibly have found out who the adopting parents were?"

"I know," Rawson said. "My father-in-law—he's dead now—never found out. What we thought was that as the woman was obviously a lady she must have had money and had bribed someone to get the information. It worried us for a bit and then the adoption went through and we forgot all about it. Till four years ago when that man arrived."

"And where's Ruth now?" Hallows asked.

"Here with us," Mrs. Rawson said. "She runs the local pony club. She's away at the moment."

"She knows she was adopted?"

She smiled. "Oh yes. We told her as soon as she was of an age to know."

"And she's never worried her head about who her parents might have been?"

"Never. It never changed her in the slightest degree."

About ten minutes later we left. They'd wanted us to stay to tea but we'd told them we really had to get back to town. Just into the main lane I drew the car up. Such an anger was gripping me that I didn't trust myself to drive. There's no anger quite like the kind that's stirred by impotence and frustration and a knowledge of absolute futility. I think I clenched my fists. I wanted to smash something. I wanted to do I didn't know what. The anger so gripped me that for quite a few moments I couldn't speak.

"I know how you feel," Hallows said quietly. "I feel the same way myself."

It was he who took the wheel. After a few minutes we began to talk. There was the reconstruction. Since the daughter's birth wasn't registered, Templett had guessed at once from that and the age of the Rawsons that it was the matter of an adoption. After that, all he'd had to do was string me along. Such an opportunity had never perhaps presented itself with Tom Jordan: working for another agency and someone who'd looked as gullible as myself had given him his chance.

What he'd done was to put up at a Norwich hotel and operate at his leisure from there. The advertisement in the local paper was a blind: the Rawsons hadn't seen it in any case. He knew where to find them and he did the necessary reconnoitring. I'd given Tom Jordan the name of the client, so Templett must have induced a colleague to find it on the time-sheet. He'd arranged with someone to get into the Strand apartment and obtain a photograph and he'd had one made of Eva Strand as she'd been at the time of her honeymoon. And so to the actual blackmail.

No wonder Eva Strand had raved at me like a mad woman. I'd promised her absolute secrecy, whereas I'd used the facts and what had been discovered to extort money. Maybe too, after the payment, she'd been told that it was only on account. That had been the final tilt towards suicide.

But what could we now do about it? Just nothing. There lay the futility. I couldn't go to Martin Strand and tell him that before her marriage his wife had given birth to an illegitimate daughter. Surmises wouldn't soften that slur. In war-time people do strange things. Maybe she was as good as engaged to some man or other who'd been killed in action before the expected marriage. I didn't know, but knowing her, it was what I guessed. Nor could I ask Strand if, just before her tragic death, his wife had drawn a largish sum of money from her private account.

All that that meant was that nothing could be done about Templett. Not only had everything happened four years ago, but all the evidence we'd uncovered was circumstantial.

"All the same," Hallows said, "I hate the thought of Templett getting away with it."

I asked him, perhaps a trifle snappily, what he thought I was thinking.

"The least we can do," he said, "is to tell the whole thing to Jewle. If there's an opening, he can find it."

I said I'd promised the Rawsons they definitely wouldn't be pestered by anyone, not even the police. But it was an idea, all the same.

"I think I'll sleep over it," I said. "We both might have some ideas by then. If not, we might talk to Jewle."

13
INTO THIN AIR

HALLOWS had just arrived next morning when there was a call for me. At first I couldn't make out the name. Even when Bertha told me again and I knew the caller was Froden, she had to ask me twice if she should put him through.

"Good-morning, Mr. Froden," I said. "Do you want to give me a message from Mr. Cofield?"

I'd never have opened a call that way if I hadn't been wondering why it was he, and not Cofield, who was ringing me.

"Is it Mr. Travers?"

"Yes," I said. "We had quite a chat together the other evening at Scotland Yard after Mr. Hallows and I had seen you and Mr. Cofield at Hollindale."

"I know, sir," he said, "but we've been very worried—"

"Wait a minute," I said. "Who're we?"

"Me and my wife, sir. It's about Mr. Alan. Now he's gone. His bed wasn't slept in last night and all he left was a note. He didn't even take his clubs."

In any other circumstances I might have smiled. That Cofield shouldn't be playing golf was virtually the end of all things.

"You're afraid something's happened to him?"

"I don't know, sir. He's been very queer in himself the last two or three days. There was some man he was talking to on the telephone and Mary happened to hear."

"Right," I said. "Just take everything calmly. Mr. Hallows and I'll be along to see you straight away."

I wanted to know what Hallows made of it. He said he didn't know. "Depends on what we hear down there," he said. "If I had to guess, I'd say he was being threatened by someone."

"The money," I said. "The thousand pounds he was trying to raise at Pentlow House. Both the Crewes remarked on how ill he was looking. You think he was being blackmailed?"

It seemed as good an explanation as any. We looked at each other as if wanting to know what we were waiting for.

Another ten minutes and we were off. Something had told me that morning that I didn't know where I might have to spend the day, so I'd brought the car along. It's never too hard to find a parking place if you get to Broad Street before nine. But it didn't look like being so fine a trip as the one we'd taken the previous day. The spell of late autumnal weather looked like ending. The wind had turned north, and when we got out in the country there was still rime on the roads from the night's sharp frost. It was just short of eleven o'clock when I drew the car into the short Southways drive.

"Might as well use the garage," Hallows said. "We don't know how long we'll be here."

It was a chance suggestion on which an enormous deal was to hang. I turned by the side of the house and found there was ample room for another left turn. The garage door had been open and, as he left, Hallows pulled it partially back on its rollers. Froden had heard us and was waiting at the back door.

"If you don't mind coming through the kitchen, gentlemen."

I said I liked kitchens. Everyone liked kitchens. People, I said, talked about a living-room fire as the centre of a home. It was nothing of the sort. It was the kitchen.

I suppose I'd been trying to cheer him up, not that he'd looked in any way lugubrious. A relief at seeing us, yes, and then a shake or two of the head.

"If you'd really prefer to stay here then, sir, I'll call Mary. I think she's upstairs."

It was a large kitchen, spotlessly clean and beautifully warm, and hanging about it was the pleasant smell of what must have been good cooking. A kettle was gently steaming on the electric stove. There was one easy chair—doubtless that used by Froden himself—and a couple of kitchen chairs. The only thing missing was a cat.

Mary Froden came in. In one who had struck me as placidly capable of handling a situation, the look she gave us was proof enough of worry.

"Let's talk this quietly over," I said. "First of all, Mrs. Froden, you show me the note Mr. Cofield left."

It was on a sheet of Southways notepaper and she'd found it propped against a vase on the table where she'd normally have set his breakfast.

I have to go away for a few days. Will let you know where later. Probably staying with a friend. If anyone should make any enquiries you're to say that I've been called away. Nothing to worry about. Expect to be back soon. A.C.

The handwriting wasn't too legible but she said the master always wrote like that.

"Right," I said. "Tell me just what he's been like since you first thought something was wrong."

It had been his manner. He was always even-tempered: sort of equably off-hand, but during the last few days he'd been irritable and even snappy. He'd got up earlier than usual, as if he'd been unable to sleep, and he'd looked unwell. Usually, she said, he was the picture of health. Also he'd been irregular about his meals, Yesterday, she said, he'd been almost an hour late for his lunch and when she ventured to ask if he wasn't feeling himself, he'd almost snapped her head off.

"How was he with you?" I asked Froden.

Froden said he'd seen very little of him. The weather had held fine, so he hadn't had to clean the car. All the same, he couldn't help noticing the change.

"Do you mind if I suggest something, sir?"

"Please do," I said. "It's the very thing we want you to do."

"Well then, sir, we think he was worried about money. I mean that was what we thought after we'd happened to over-hear that telephone call."

Between them they told us what had happened. It was two days previously. It was as if Cofield had been expecting that call. When Mary had come in at her usual eight o'clock, Cofield was already up and asking for his breakfast. When she came to clear away, she saw he'd eaten very little, though all the coffee had been drunk. She'd asked if there'd been anything wrong with it and apparently he'd waved her impatiently away and said he just didn't feel like eating.

A minute or two later the paper arrived. When she brought it in he was sitting moodily by the telephone. He usually sat by the fire. At about nine o'clock Froden came to the kitchen to hear if there'd been any special instructions, and it was a few seconds later that they heard what they heard. Normally anything said in the lounge would have been almost inaudible but this had been shouted. Whether the words they remembered were the exact ones we couldn't tell. In any case it was the sense that mattered.

"God-dammit, I can't! I haven't got it. I haven't got it!"

That had been all. Cofield had probably realised he'd been shouting and after that nothing was heard. About two minutes later he came by the kitchen window and they heard him get out the car and drive off.

"What about yesterday?" Hallows said.

It had been a repetition of the previous day except that, if there'd been a telephone call, then Mary couldn't be positive about it. She'd been upstairs at nine o'clock and she'd thought she'd heard the telephone bell ring, but if it had, it'd been for the merest second. When she came down some ten minutes later, Cofield had gone out, but this time he hadn't taken the car.

Something else had happened during the afternoon. Cofield had mentioned to Froden that he'd be playing with Major Lovell, and after lunch he'd gone out, presumably to the clubhouse. At about three o'clock he'd come back. Mary said she hadn't expected him and when would he like tea. He said he wouldn't be wanting tea and he probably wouldn't be in again till late. If he wasn't in before seven she wasn't to expect him. And that was the last either of the Frodens heard or saw of him.

"Did he take a bag with him when he left last night?"

"Yes, sir. He took a big white bag he had and a lot of his clothes. I was upstairs trying to find out just what when you arrived."

"What was funny was about his golf bag," Froden said. "When he came in yesterday afternoon he brought it with him.

I thought he'd be wanting me to clean his clubs as I often do, but the bag's still there."

It was at that moment that I saw the man.

From the kitchen window above the sink you can see along the drive to where it turns to meet the main drive-in to the club-house. I'd got up to stretch my legs and I happened to be looking out. The man was fairly tall and heavily built and he was wearing a dark overcoat and a bowler. His hands were in the overcoat pockets.

I can't pin down the precise thing that made me suspicious. Perhaps it was a lot of things: the curious atmosphere in that kitchen where we'd been talking about curious things, and the way the man seemed to be peering about. He'd paused for a moment some twenty yards from the house and gave a quick look in the direction of the garage. And he was walking. He had no car.

"You're having a caller," I said. "Get to the door, Mary, and find out what he wants."

I drew Hallows towards the back door. "Slip round by the back," I said, "and see if there's a car parked anywhere near. When he comes back, try and get a good look at him. It may be nothing but you never know."

I waited in the kitchen till Mary came back. It must have been quite ten minutes. Froden had said he was most likely a man trying to sell something. But he wasn't.

He'd asked if Mr. Cofield was in and was told he'd been called away. She didn't know where and it hadn't been her place to ask questions. The man had been quietly persistent. Mr. Cofield, he said, should have met him the previous night on an important business matter but hadn't turned up. The matter was so important that he'd come all the way from London to see him. Was she sure she didn't know where he might be found? Hadn't she any suggestions? Was she married? Might her husband know?

She must have handled the situation remarkably well. What finally happened was that he gave her a telephone number and a pound note. She was to ring the number as soon as Mr. Cofield returned or as soon as she knew where he was. He hinted that there'd be a much bigger tip if she kept the matter strictly to herself.

She asked if she'd done right to take the money. I said it was the best thing she could have done. She gave me the telephone number. It was written on a page torn from a small notebook.

"You think he was telling the truth, sir?"

"I don't think so," I said. "We may know a bit more when Mr. Hallows gets back."

He came in almost at once. He hadn't been able to get a good look at the man but he'd taken the number of the car, a blue and cream Zodiac. The car had been parked on the main road just short of the drive-in and it was headed in the direction of town. The man had driven off at quite a good lick and it didn't look as if he had any intention of coming back.

I asked Mary what the man's voice had been like. Had he sounded like a gentleman?

"No, sir," she said. "I wouldn't say he was. He hadn't the right way with him, if you know what I mean."

I thought things over for a moment, then said we ought perhaps to have a word with Major Lovell. She glanced up at the kitchen clock. She flushed slightly as she said she wasn't trying to drive us away but if we were any time at the club-house, mightn't she be getting us some lunch? Just a cold lunch. It wouldn't take any time to prepare. I said that was very good of her and we'd be glad to accept.

We stopped at the entrance to the car-park to talk things briefly over. Cofield, we decided, was definitely being black-mailed. He'd been ordered to have a thousand pounds ready and was told to wait till nine the next morning when he'd be given further instructions. Those instructions, given yesterday morning, had been to bring the money to town that night. Cofield hadn't been able to raise the money. He'd pretended to agree and then he'd bolted.

"But what had he to fear?" Hallows said. "If everything we were told was true, then why the blackmail?"

I said there was only one answer. What he'd told us was either very wrong or very incomplete.

We moved on to the club-house. Major Lovell was working away in his office. He recognised Hallows at once.

"You're the fellow who had to pay Alan Cofield half-a-crown."

Hallows admitted it. He introduced me and said we'd been hoping to see Cofield but he'd suddenly gone away on some business or other. Lovell looked interested.

"That's not like him. Wonder why he didn't mention it yesterday afternoon." He suddenly remembered something. "He isn't ill, is he? Gone off to see a doctor or something?"

"Why do you think he was ill?"

"Well, he hasn't been looking well the last day or two. Also he broke off the game yesterday afternoon. Said he wasn't feeling too fit and would I mind if he turned it in. We only played the first nine. Never knew him play such utter rubbish. Couldn't hit a ball."

We took our time getting back to the house. It was half-past twelve when we'd finished a couple of drinks with Lovell. Mary had laid lunch in the lounge—cold ham and a salad, boiled potatoes, cheese and a couple of bottles of beer. She and Froden, she said, would be having theirs in the kitchen.

There wasn't any great hurry, so we took our time. It was getting on for two o'clock when we asked Froden to come in. What we wanted him to do was go over again in detail everything that had happened after he and his wife had got back on that Sunday night from their day at Newhurst. It was only towards the end of his story that we found a discrepancy.

"Think very carefully," I said. "It's highly important. You heard Mr. Cofield take out his car about ten minutes after you heard another car drive away. You say it was a long time after that when Mr. Cofield came back."

He explained. He was a light sleeper. The vital time was half-past twelve. If Cofield had come back earlier than that and driven the car into the garage, then he'd definitely have heard it. What he'd heard at twelve-thirty was the sound of a car. It was as if it'd been coming towards the house, and then apparently it had stopped. In the morning he was always awake by six and it was shortly after that that Cofield had driven the car into the garage.

There was no point in showing him we were any further interested. We thanked him and that was that.

"Cofield was lying," Hallows said. "His statement was that he'd thought of chasing the other car and then had changed his mind and come home. He didn't actually get back till half-past twelve. He didn't want Froden to know what time it really was, so he left the car well short of the house and garaged it early next morning. Probably told Froden he'd left it standing in front of the house all night."

I did a quick bit of thinking. "I don't know about you but I'm getting a whole lot of ideas."

"Such as?"

I told him to listen to what I was going to tell Jewle.

Jewle was in.

"Hallows and I are at Cofield's place," I said. "There've been a whole lot of developments. Can't tell you what now but we'll be with you in just over an hour. Got your pad ready? There's a thing or two I'd like you to take down."

I gave him the number of the blue and cream Zodiac and asked him to trace the owner. I gave him the telephone number Mary Froden had been given.

"One other thing. Cofield's car is an off-white M.G.: registration number BHY 127. I suggest you get a reliable man out to Ludwold, Helen Vaile's place. It's just possible the car may be in her garage. Tell you all about it when we see you."

I rang off. Hallows said I just might be right. The Grand Alliance, as he called them—Caroline Daunt, Helen Vaile and Cofield himself. Then he had an idea.

"Let's just suppose. Those three are tied in together. It's something we agreed on. Cofield may be Caroline's boyfriend. What I'm getting at is this. The blackmailer has something on Cofield, so why shouldn't he have something on the other two? Why not ring Mrs. Daunt, for instance, and hear what she sounds like? Make it up as you go along."

I didn't have to make anything up. I hadn't given myself credit for being so meticulous, but I found Caroline Daunt's number in my notebook.

"You wished to speak to Mrs. Daunt?" asked the operator at the apartments' exchange.

"I did," I said. "Isn't she available?"

"No, sir: she's away. She won't be back for a few days."

"Curious," I said. "Did she leave this morning?"

"Yesterday afternoon."

"I'm a very old friend," I said, "and I have to get into touch with her. Did she say where you were to forward her letters?"

"Mrs. Daunt didn't want them forwarded," she told me patiently.

"But what about the funeral?"

"Mr. Daunt's funeral was yesterday morning," she told me. And rang off.

I was smiling a bit ruefully. I'd claimed to be a friend but hadn't known about the funeral. Not that it mattered. What did matter was that Caroline Daunt, like Cofield, had decided to get out of circulation.

A few minutes later we were on our way. As I drove the car out of the garage I couldn't help thinking how lucky that suggestion of Hallows had been. Had the car been left in front of the house, the caller could have taken its number. Even the sight of it would have told him the Frodens had a visitor or visitors. He could have waited till we'd gone and then had a good look at us. We didn't know him but there was just the chance that he might have recognised us.

Hallows was saying something. "Do you know, I felt a bit cock-a-hoop when we learned that the Daunt woman had gone. Now I'm not so sure. She might have gone somewhere just to get over things. Didn't want anyone to know where because she didn't want to be pestered."

"And Cofield?"

"Well, you have to try all angles," he told me. "There *is* just the chance that he was avoiding some creditor or other. What about a gambling debt? Those boys can play it pretty rough. They'd scare the living daylights out of anyone like Cofield."

I had to admit he was right.

"Why not stick to the optimistic side?" I said. "Why not go the whole hog? Cofield and the Daunt woman have skipped it for the same reason—the jewellery."

"Then what scared them? Who could have known they had anything to do with it? We've been working on it for best part of a fortnight and still can't prove a thing."

"Daunt's death," I said. "That's what scared 'em. It shouldn't have happened. It threw the spanner into the works. And it happened in the wrong place."

If it didn't convince him, at least it gave him something to think about. In any case, we were now in the traffic stream and there was little more talking. And both of us felt, I think, that by the time our talk with Jewle was ended, we'd have a far clearer view. We didn't know how long that talk was going to be.

14
PLAN OF CAMPAIGN

IT WAS one of the longest sessions I'd ever sat through, and when it was half-past six and it looked as if we'd scarcely started, I rang the flat and said I couldn't get home till late.

It was a question of one thing leading to another. I'll try to sort it out, not that things will necessarily be in the right order. What happened was that I was all agog to hear who owned the Zodiac and whose number Mary Froden was supposed to ring.

"The car," he said, and looked at his pad. "It's registered in the name of a Frederick Templett of 32 Priory Road, Bethnal Green. The same man has the telephone number. He's a car dealer. And now suppose you tell us a few things."

"Just one moment," I said. "Have you anything on this Frederick Templett?"

"Nothing that stuck. Two years ago he was questioned in connection with a stolen car but he seems to have wriggled clear. Why d'you ask? You know him?"

You see where that led us. As soon as I said it'd be a very long story, he had a stenographer in. Something was telling me that this time I'd little to gain by keeping anything back, so I began straightaway with the Eva Strand case. I carried it on to the time of its abandonment. Then came the ticklish part.

"You remember my telling you how Caroline Daunt had lied to her husband about having been all day in the apartment when I'd seen her in Regent Street with a man? Possibly I didn't tell you who that man was. It didn't seem necessary, but it was Geoff Templett."

He gave me a quick look.

"That's right," I said. "Presumably brother of the Frederick Templett whose car you traced."

You see what had to happen? Off at a tangent again. Geoff Templett had to be side-tracked while we told about that morning's visit to Hollindale. This time Hallows did the talking and again nothing was left out: Cofield's appearance, the telephone call, the golf bag, Major Lovell, the left note—the lot. I admit that Hallows by accident or design left out the discrepancy in Cofield's account of that late Sunday night, but even that was to be brought in later.

"And what'd you make of it all?"

"We fined it down to two things," Hallows told him. "Either Cofield was being blackmailed or else he'd got in deep with someone. Might be a gambling set."

"Wait a minute," Jewle said. "If he was being blackmailed, what about?"

Hallows' shrug of the shoulders was as good as a you-tell-me. I put in my pennyworth.

"Daunt's death took place in the vicinity. Cofield may know more about it than he ever admitted. Come to think of it, he did."

Off at a tangent again. Jewle opened a drawer of his desk and brought out a thickish file.

"Here's Cofield's signed statement. He guessed that the caller had been sent by Daunt and wondered why, and then he decided to find out. He went after him in his car but it was a bad night for driving so he turned back. He probably wasn't away from the house for more than a quarter of an hour. According to Froden, that's all wrong."

I repeated Froden's statement to us. Jewle said it sounded like the truth.

"Away for two hours," he said. "What the devil was he doing for the whole two hours?"

He thought of something. You can always tell when Jewle has a hunch. He has the trick of half-raising his hand and cocking his index finger as if he's about to point something out.

"Helen Vaile," he said. "What made you suggest Cofield might have gone to her place?"

"Almost the last time I saw you, we agreed those three looked as if they might be mixed up in something together. Hallows here, called them The Grand Alliance. Caroline Daunt is the third. Remember that Cofield knew Vaile. He was the one who talked to her the day she went to Pentlow House on what we know to have been false pretences. He lied about the length of his talk with her. Cofield's just the type to've let the meeting blossom a bit further. She's far from an unattractive woman. Which reminds me. When I asked him about her, he tried to make out she was a kind of journalistic hag."

Before he could speak, I thought of something else. "Did you know Caroline Daunt left her apartment yesterday without leaving any address?"

"Oh, yes," he said. "The superintendent let me know." He smiled dryly. "Don't tell me she's gone to the Vaile woman too?"

"Far more unlikely things. You did send a man down there?"

"I had a call from him just before you arrived. The garage hasn't any windows and it's locked. And there's room for only one car. We can't make an entry till there's sufficient evidence. He may be able to overhear people talking inside the house."

He made as if to put the file back in its drawer, then thought of something else.

"That Eva Strand case you were telling me about. I don't see the point of it. You had to drop it when she committed suicide, but what's that to do with all this business?"

Off we went again. I told him about the McGuffie letter and how it had made us review that four-year-old case. I told him everything that had happened when we'd seen the Rawsons. He sat very still when at last I'd finished.

"The bastard!" he said quietly. "The double-dealing bastard! And you're going to let him get away with it!"

"Think of Martin Strand," I said. "He lost his daughter, then his wife. It'd be inhuman to rake it all up again. And he's the only real witness. He's the only one who could say if his wife drew out any money."

H clicked his tongue annoyedly.

"I can't make you people out. Sometimes you can see through a ten-inch wall and then you can't see what's under your noses. It isn't what happened four years ago. It's the use that can be made of it. You got a picture of Geoff Templett?"

I said I hadn't, but Tom Jordan would probably have one in his files.

"Right," he said. "I suggest that first thing in the morning, you see him. If the picture's good enough, you see the Rawsons again and get Templett identified. I'll send Matthews with you. There'd better be an official statement."

He saw the quick alarm. "Everything will be done discreetly. And later you'll have to identify the brother. That'll also mean an official statement from Mrs. Froden. Mr. Hallows had better see to that, if he doesn't mind. Another twenty-four hours and there ought to be enough to get a warrant."

I didn't altogether like it but I had to agree. He wanted to know if there was anything else.

"Right," he said. "We might as well have a bite of something while everything gets typed."

Sandwiches and coffee came up while we were stretching our legs. I was looking forward to the coffee. After all that talking, my throat felt like an old fur rug. But there was more talking to come. Luckily it was Jewle this time who did most of it.

"You might like to know about Daunt's will," he said. "There's something very significant about it, especially the date it was made. It was a Tuesday, wasn't it, when you people met in John Hill's office?"

"That's right. Guy Fawkes Day."

"Well, Daunt saw his solicitors and altered his will the very next day. He wanted a quick completion and it was ready to be signed two days later. I ought to explain that old John Parwell left the business entirely to him in a will made just after Caroline married Daunt. Daunt's will left the business to Bendale. Caroline got a thousand a year from the business as long as she remained unmarried."

"Good Lord," I said. "He knew she was playing around with some other man?"

"Could be," he said. "I'd like to think it was something else. What if he had a good idea—after that meeting with John Hill—that she'd been involved in the jewellery substitution."

I didn't know what to say. It certainly made one think.

"You see the irony of it?" Jewle asked us. "Let's suppose she did the job somehow or found a way for someone else to do it. She wanted to get rid of Daunt but she'd also want money. You see the point?"

We did. The irony was that she couldn't have known that Daunt was going to be killed. Once he was dead, she'd have had money. John Parwell would have dropped clean in her lap. All the intrigues that had culminated in the substitution had resulted in the loss of a flourishing business and the gain of a paltry thousand a year. Even her cut from what a fence paid wouldn't make up for what would have been—as the solicitors had let fall—somewhere about seven thousand a year.

The buzzer went. It was Jewle's man speaking from Ludwold. The light was still on in Helen Vaile's lounge and there'd been the tapping of a typewriter. No voices.

"Wait till she goes to bed," Jewle told him, "and then get back here."

Before he could tell us what exactly he had in mind, the typed statements came in. They weren't official, of course: merely the material with which he'd work, but they had to be checked almost paragraph by paragraph in case anything had been missed. It was getting on for ten o'clock by the time we'd finished. Jewle looked a bit tired, which wasn't very usual, or should I have said faint but pursuing. He was actually thinking of ringing the Rawsons to warn them we'd be coming. I told him there'd be plenty of time in the morning.

I began working out my own times. All he wanted to know was when Matthews should pick me up. According to the schedule he'd worked out for me, I said it might be as well if we started straight away.

He laughed. If I hadn't been putting on my overcoat and well out of arms' reach, I think he'd have clapped me on the back.

"Think of that fat fee you're going to collect from John Hill."

Hallows gave him a quick look. "What makes you optimistic all of a sudden?"

"Me?" Jewle said. "You're the ones who ought to be optimistic. Look what you've uncovered."

"Depends what you read into it," I said. "Maybe you've spotted something we've missed."

I won't go so far as to say that I can read Jewle's mind. What I can sometimes do is guess the direction in which he's heading, and it seemed to me that he was just about to produce some flippancy or other and then as suddenly he changed his mind.

"We've all been pretty busy today," he said, "and I'm like you fellows—off for a few hours sleep. What I don't think I'm going to get out of my mind, though, is what you told me about Templett and the Daunt woman. There's something important there if we could only just find it."

He broke off. "Ah, well: won't keep you people any longer. Ten o'clock suit you for Matthews?"

Hallows and I had a word at the car. Jewle, we agreed, had read into what he'd heard that night something important which we ought to have seized on ourselves. And since he wasn't one to play tricks, he was probably sure that we'd soon be finding it ourselves. Was he thinking that something we were going to do the next day would throw light on it?

"The relationships between Templett and Mrs. Daunt," I said. Then I grunted. "All he's done is think of a way to keep me awake half the night."

It didn't turn out to be as bad as that. Before I at last went to sleep—and that was after only about an hour—I did go over the various connections between Templett and Caroline Daunt from the first moment they'd met. There hadn't been a tremendous deal to think about when you cut out the surmise and kept to fact: just her divorce, the meeting in Regent Street and the threats.

It was the very paucity of facts that kept leading me astray. I've sometimes thought that hanging above my office desk there ought to be a pictorial representation of Naaman the Syrian. You remember him. In his country were rivers that made Jordan look like a trickle. He wanted something grandiose to bathe in. What the prophet had told him really hurt his dignity. That's how I was, and often am. I have facts but they're too simple. So I expand them. I make labyrinthine ideas in which to lose myself, and it's only when I discard them on the way back that I come across the sign-post that says "This Way Out".

That was how it was when I woke next morning. My mind was clear. The few facts from which I'd started the previous night were now as clear as the air of that early morning. A couple of minutes and there the whole thing was.

I rang Tom Jordan at his private address and said I'd be at his office on a matter of urgent business at nine. I didn't tell him the Eva Strand story. What I said in his office was that Templett had over-reached himself and the police thought they had a case, and, since my firm was involved, they'd asked if I could furnish a photograph. He had one: just what I wanted. A glossy head-and-shoulders of the Templett of 1957.

Matthews and I had a perfectly smooth time with the Rawsons. Jewle had told them that, whatever happened to Templett, nothing whatever concerning them or Ruth would ever be made public. They were nice people. I'd never have forgiven Jewle if by force of circumstances he'd had to break his word. The official business wasn't over till after one and they insisted on us staying to lunch.

We changed course on the way back and shifted south to Woodford and Stratford and then to Bethnal Green. Priory Road took a bit of finding out. Once we were in it, we soon found Fred Templett's place. We drove on a hundred yards or so and parked in a side street. Matthews stayed in the car.

The Bethnal Green Car Mart was garage and car mart combined. It hadn't been modernised. To the left as I approached it was a bombed lot on which some thirty cars were displayed, each with a price prominent on the windshield. The garage was an old building that might have served as a smallish warehouse. By its arched entrance were two pumps close to the wall and set back from the pavement. The interior was a bit gloomy. A hatchet-faced mechanic of about forty was working on the engine of an oldish Rover. Just beyond him, the blue and cream Zodiac was parked close to the wall.

"You the boss?"

He straightened himself. "No, sir. He's about somewhere. He might be in the office."

He was pointing away to my left. I tapped at the door and was told to come in. Fred Templett looked quickly up and got as quickly to his feet. It was as if the look he'd given me had furnished him with the whole of my history.

"Good-afternoon, sir. What can I do for you?"

I gave him a card. It said I was J.W. Waters, of Waters and Drew, Chartered Accountants; Headquarters, Chelmsford. I said I'd had business in the neighbourhood and had happened to notice his cars. My own car was temporarily in dry dock: a 1960 Mark 2 Jaguar which I was thinking of turning in for a Mark 4. Good second-hand would suit me as well as new. Subject, of course, to an A.A. vetting.

He was smooth. He'd have made an admirable spieler for a television commercial: his voice had that essential unctuosity. He saw my position. Not that he cared overmuch for the Mark 4. But it did so happen that he knew of one: owner-driven and only fifteen thousand on the clock. I wouldn't prefer a Zodiac? And so on for another five minutes. He'd get into touch at the earliest possible moment. If he saw a chance of acquiring the Jaguar, maybe I'd prefer him to let me see it at Chelmsford. Some of that was on the way out, but he steered me in the direction of the Zodiac and mentioned it almost casually as we went by.

"He's our man?" Matthews asked me as I got into the car.

I said there wasn't a doubt. He was the one who'd been looking for Cofield at Hollindale.

Jewle wasn't in when we got back to the Yard. Hallows, we learned, was back from Hollindale with Mary Froden's statement, but he'd long since gone.

"What now?" I said.

"Go home and put your feet up," he told me. "I doubt if there'll be anything doing before the morning. There's bound to be a conference later on. If the Old Man needs you, he'll give you a ring."

I suppose I could have asked for a car, but I made my own way to Broad Street. Hallows was there. Over a belated cup of tea we talked about our day. I asked if he had thought any more about that hint which Jewle had dropped the previous night. He said he had and he hadn't. He'd been dog-tired the previous night and busy the next morning.

"You know what I think Jewle spotted?" I said. "Something about Caroline Daunt's divorce."

He didn't see it.

"Listen," I said. "There's nothing whatever we knew that Jewle didn't know by the time we were ready to leave last night. He was even told how Templett and Caroline got acquainted and how her divorce was worked."

"Wait a minute," he said. "I'm beginning to see something. You mean the way Templett rigged things so as to find the boxer with a woman in the flat?"

"That's it," I said. "That's the vital thing. So let's start supposing. Templett had had Caroline followed: otherwise he wouldn't have known about the boy-friend. When he threatened her, he really meant it, and this is what may have happened."

Templett, I said, had seen her with Cofield, and he knew who Cofield was and where he lived. After the threats he got into touch with Daunt. If Daunt had proved by enquiries at the desk that his wife had been lying about being all day in the flat, then he'd be in a receptive mood. It had been agreed that Daunt should ostensibly arrange a trip to Edinburgh and the moment Caroline left the flat on the Saturday, Templett had her watched. He saw her arrive at Ludwold and later he saw Cofield arrive quite late in his car and take her to Hollindale. He rang Daunt. He rang him again on the Sunday morning. From the departure of the Frodens he'd judged that she'd be there another night.

Daunt left as if for Edinburgh and rendezvoused with Templett. The same trick that had exposed the boxer was going to be tried out again. It might have been Fred Templett who made the actual call while his brother and Daunt stayed in the car. All that was necessary was to flush the couple out. As soon as Cofield and the lady left the house, they'd have been pounced on.

"What went wrong?"

"Don't know," I said. "Maybe Daunt didn't like the way things were being handled and there was an argument and they had to put the body in the car and get rid of it. But we do know what Cofield did. As soon as he thought the coast was clear, he rushed Caroline back to Ludwold."

"You're right," Hallows said. "No wonder Daunt's death put a spanner into the works."

"And hence the blackmailing. If the death was accidental and Templett and his brother thought they could prove it—if they ever had to—then they were sitting pretty after all. They had a couple of people to blackmail. They could accuse each of them of having been concerned in Daunt's death. Neither Cofield nor the lady was in a position to disprove it."

Hallows agreed. "You think Jewle spotted the similarity?"

"Maybe," I said. "All I know now is I ought to've spotted it myself."

We weren't cock-a-hoop for long. Something occurred to both of us at the same time.

"You know what we've done?" Hallows said. "We've been sweating blood working for Jewle. He doesn't give a damn about the jewellery business. His pigeon was the Daunt killing. So where does that leave us?"

I didn't quite know, but I wasn't inclined to be so pessimistic.

"What about your famous Grand Alliance?" I said. "The one thing that could have united those three was the jewellery. We've helped Jewle: now he'll help us. As soon as he can lay hands on Cofield and the lady he can have them on the grill."

"You're forgetting something. Just where are they? For all we know, both or either might be over the water. Once those stones are disposed of, there'll be no getting them back. We get paid our time, but we lose a five per-cent bonus."

"You know Jewle," I said. "He never says a single word more than he has to. If Cofield really is at Ludwold, he'll have the place under observation."

"No harm in giving him a ring. He might be back by now."

He was back.

"No need for you people to worry," he told me quietly. "Everything's under control, even at the Vaile place. We don't know what's in the garage but we do know that her car isn't. She took it two days ago to the local garage and asked them to service it while she was away. This morning she cancelled the milk and the newspaper."

I hope he didn't hear the sigh of relief.

"You'll be wanting us in the morning?"

"Don't know yet," he said. "I'm due for a conference in a few minutes, so it all depends. I'll give you a ring in the morning if that'll be all right."

15
DEAD MAN'S WORDS

MATTHEWS rang me shortly after eight the next morning. He wanted to know if I could identify the Crewe jewellery. For a moment I couldn't believe my ears.

"You've recovered it?"

"No, no," he said. "All we think is there may be a good chance of recovering it. Possibly this morning. Of course we'd have to prove unlawful possession and that's where you'd come in."

I told him I could do the job as well as anybody except Julia Crewe. She'd seen the originals. All I'd seen were the replicas, and very good replicas they were.

"Sounds good enough. Could you be here at about nine?"

I drove down. Matthews was waiting for me in a police car.

"Going somewhere, are we?"

"That's right," he said. "X is the spot where two lines meet."

The car was heading west. I asked where Jewle was. He said he might possibly be joining us later. At the moment he was at the control point.

"What's all this geometric gibberish?" I said. "Have you people passed a law or something about straight answers to straight questions?"

He laughed. "Just trying it on. Seeing if you could puzzle it out."

I wouldn't have puzzled it out in a month of Sundays. What had been happening was this. As soon as Jewle was reasonably sure that a move from Ludwold was intended, enquiries were made at London Airport and Gatwick and the leading agencies. It was discovered that two tickets on the ten o'clock plane to Paris from London Airport had been purchased in the names of Helen Vaile and Caroline Daunt. The real names had had to be used or there'd have been trouble with passports.

"Now I get you," I said. "We're converging on London Airport and so is Vaile."

"That's right. Just after I phoned you, word came through from Ludwold that Vaile and a man—presumably Cofield—had just left in Cofield's car. Soon as we knew they were going due south, I went down to wait for you."

"But it's no distance from Ludwold. What is it? Eighteen miles."

"No panic," he told me. "They'll be met. They don't know it, but they'll be under observation soon as they get near the airport."

"What about Cofield? If he hasn't got a ticket, is he going to take up an available seat?"

"Don't know," he said. "But what we've got to remember is that these people aren't running away from us. As far as they know we aren't interested. The one they're running away from is the blackmailer. They've had to scheme all this because they haven't a notion who he is."

I said he was right but what interested me was the fact that the jewels were probably being taken too. He chuckled.

"They have to pay expenses, don't they? But seriously, there's no need to worry. It doesn't matter if they get there before us. Everything's under control. What's being done is to query the passports. That'll hold 'em up."

As he said, the three had been free as air—as far as concerned the telephone. They'd been in regular communication with plenty of time to make their plans. Caroline Daunt, whose description was near enough to that of the purchaser of the tickets, had most likely been staying at a hotel in town.

We were drawing into the airport. Matthews told the driver to slow down. Just round the corner at the end of the long bend the car drew in. I recognised the sergeant whom I'd more than once seen with Jewle. Matthews got out.

A short conference, and the sergeant got in with us. His name was Miller. Cofield and Vaile had arrived, Matthews told me. A medium-sized suitcase had been taken from the boot and the woman was carrying a largish handbag. A minute or two later, Cofield had left in the car. He wouldn't know he was being followed.

The three of us went to Security. Matthews and Miller did some conferring with a couple of men: Security, probably, or they might have been Customs. I didn't know. I'd been parked in an easy chair some distance away. When the four of them went out, Matthews told me to sit tight. He oughtn't to be more than a few minutes.

A charming secretary brought me some magazines. She asked if I'd like coffee and I said I would. She ordered it on the intercom. Maybe she'd been ordered to keep me there, you never know with Matthews.

In any case I sat there. They'd done me proud, with a small pot of coffee and not just a cup. When I'd finished it I lighted my pipe. A quarter of an hour and I was still there. Every now and again the secretary would catch my eye and give me what I took for a reassuring smile. Ten more minutes and Matthews really came back.

"All clear," he said. "Nothing to do but make the identification. Don't think you'll have any difficulty. They look the real thing to me."

We went along a corridor and turned right into another. Outside was the din of planes, and people were moving across the tarmac. We went through a door into what looked like a small waiting room. Miller was there and the two men who'd accompanied Matthews. Matthews introduced me. I wasn't doing a lot of listening. I was looking at the three dark-green cases on the table. I didn't even wait to be asked to open them.

And there it was. The Crewe jewellery. And intact. The stones hadn't been prised out. I'd seen plenty of jewellery in my time but this was really something. That small tiara was as fine as anything I'd seen. The necklace I didn't like so much but what really took my breath away were the two earrings nestling in their case: two beautifully set stones that must have been eight carats each.

"What about it?" Matthews was asking.

"It's the real thing," I said, and still a bit bemused. "If necessary I can swear it's the Crewe jewellery."

Matthews chuckled. "That's that then. If you don't mind going with Miller. Just a few things to clear up and I'll be with you in no time."

Miller and I went back to the car. While we were waiting, he told me what had happened. The two women hadn't been together, which meant two separate and identical operations: the query about the passport, the taking to a room apart, presumably for a short enquiry, and then the announcement that there'd have to be a search.

"Plenty of indignation?"

"Don't know, sir. I wasn't there but I gather they almost had to put 'em in straightjackets. The short one had two cases sewn in her corset and the other woman had one. I think it was the one with the two earrings."

The women were still there. Matthews was probably arranging about getting them to the Yard. It was twenty minutes before he joined us. As the car moved off I asked him what had happened to the jewellery. He grinned as he tapped the breast pocket of his overcoat.

"Good lord! Do you know what you've got there? They're insured for best part of fifty thousand pounds!" He laughed. "What d'you expect? An armoured car?" His face sobered a bit too quickly. "Why shouldn't the three of us make a bolt for it? Sixteen thousand apiece isn't to be sneezed at."

He answered his own question.

"Maybe you're right. Better play it the straight way."

"That's right," I told him. "Virtue triumphant. And think what you'll be able to tell your grandchildren."

Jewle's eyes popped a bit too when he saw that jewellery. He'd already been notified from the airport about its recovery. Matthews had left again. Cofield had gone straight to a roadhouse hotel near Maidenhead and Matthews was off to pick him up. Jewle asked if Matthews had told me about Hallows.

"What about him?" I said.

"Ah!" he said. "Something we thought of. Operation Fred Templett. I got hold of Hallows early this morning and he went down to Hollindale. He's on his way back now."

Jewle had thought rightly that Hallows was the one person who could get Mary Froden to do the job. There'd have to be the right words and the right tone of voice. What had happened was that she'd rung the number, given her name and had said she'd heard from Mr. Cofield. He was staying at the Bamford Hotel, Knightsbridge. Templett had thanked her and said she'd get what he'd promised. He'd put it straight away in the post.

"Everything's fixed up at the hotel," Jewle said. "Entry in the hotel register, what's to be done about the key and so on. When Templett calls—and I think he'll have to—he'll find a couple of my men in the room."

There was nothing to do but wait. I wanted to know if either of the women had done any talking and he said they hadn't. They'd be kept strictly apart as they'd been at the airport. Neither would know what'd happened to the other. Cofield would be kept apart too, and he wouldn't know what'd happened to the two women.

"What about the other Templett?"

"It depends," he said. "We'd like to pick up Fred in the hotel room. If we do, then we'll pick up Geoff. I'd rather like to be in on that myself. I expect you would too."

He said he had a search warrant. What he'd do was impound all Templett's files and try to find out if the firm had been a cover for any more blackmail. He said it might be a long and ticklish business.

It was after twelve o'clock and he suggested a bite while we had the time. Sandwiches and beer came up. Matthews rang from Maidenhead to say he was just about to start back with Cofield. Cofield was scared out of his wits, he said. It wouldn't need much pressure to make him talk. Then there was a call from the hotel to say that Templett still hadn't shown up.

"I wouldn't worry," Jewle told me. "He's probably calculating that Cofield'll be in for lunch."

I mentioned in what I thought a rather subtle way that theory Hallows had arrived at: the one about the catching of Cofield and Caroline Daunt more or less in *flagrante delicto*.

The one that had been employed in the Gannon case. Sure enough he'd worked it out.

"It just struck me there might be a similarity of procedure. What's worked well once is worth trying a second time. Not that we can prove it—not yet. We've enough to hold both the Templetts and one of them's bound to break, especially if we scare 'em with a capital charge."

He asked if I'd like to give the news about the jewellery to John Hill and the Crewes. I rang Pentlow House first but the Crewes were lunching out, so I left a message with Robert. Hill was in and I'd rarely heard him more excited. He wanted to know where the jewellery was. Jewle had a few words with him. He said we might be seeing him later in the day.

It was five minutes past one when the telephone went. Jewle reached for it. He nodded once or twice.

"Right," he said. "You know what you have to do."

"Fred Templett," he said. "He was just approaching the desk. They'll say the key's still there, so Cofield's in his room."

We sat there and we didn't say a word. Jewle got up and walked across to the window. My pipe was out so I lighted it again. That's the only tension there ever is in a case—just when you hope it's nearing its end. And mercifully we didn't have long to wait. It was only about five minutes later that the buzzer went again. Jewle was across like a flash.

"Yes?" he said, and listened. "That's fine. Couldn't be better. Charge him with intent to do grievous bodily harm."

He was grinning as he put back the receiver. "Templett walked clean into it. You know what he had on him? A short cosh and a set of knuckle-dusters. The jagged edge type."

I think I winced. If Cofield had been there he'd have ended up as a nasty mess.

Jewle was making for his hat and coat. "Right," he said. "Let's go and have a word with brother Geoff."

Years ago I sometimes mentioned a curious anticipatory look that used to appear on the face of a certain Chief-Superintendent with whom I used to work—the look of a Colosseum lion who's just espied a particularly plump Christian. That was just how Jewle was looking then.

The two men who had been keeping Templett's agency under observation were waiting some fifty yards short by the kerb. Templett, they said, was still in. He'd arrived just after nine that morning and hadn't stirred since. There was a space by a parking meter just past the door.

"Right," Jewle said. "We'll leave the car there and go in together."

The agency was on the first floor of a smallish office block. Just across from the lift was the door: on the frosted glass of the upper half was CONFIDENTIAL ENQUIRIES LTD. lettered neatly in black. Jewle motioned to his men to stay well to the side, then he knocked.

A youngish-looking secretary-receptionist, little more than a teenager, opened the door. Jewle's voice was quiet; almost confidential.

"Is Geoff in?"

"You mean Mr. Templett?"

"Of course," Jewle said. "We haven't an appointment. Just two old friends who want to give him a surprise. It's through there, isn't it?"

She hardly knew what to make of it. In any case we were inside. Jewle smiled. He waved a finger as if for silence and we moved across to the far door. He didn't knock: he just went through.

Templett must have heard us in the reception room. He couldn't have been all that busy—left hand holding down the pages of a book and the right making notes in another. Maybe that was the routine for impressing a client: that and the quizzical smile as he got to his feet. He caught sight of me and the smile went.

"Hallo, Templett," I said. "Nice place you've got here. Sorry I haven't been able to drop in before."

The smile came back. "That's all right. Nice to see you, Mr. Travers. You're looking well."

"You too," I said. "This is a friend of mine. Superintendent Jewle of New Scotland Yard."

He was suddenly very still. You could almost see the question flash across his mind.

"Sorry we disturbed you," Jewle said. "Or were you just waiting for a telephone call?"

Templett forced a smile. "A telephone call?"

"That's right. From your brother. We picked him up a few minutes ago at the Bamford Hotel. He's been charged with intent to do grievous bodily harm. I'd like you to accompany us to the Yard to answer a few questions."

"No, sir." He raised a hand. "I've nothing to do with what my brother does. As a matter of fact, we haven't been friendly for years."

"Nice to hear it," Jewle said. "But it's not only that. We think you may be able to help us in the matter of an attempted blackmail on an Alan Cofield. There's also the matter of the death of a Stephen Daunt."

"I want to ring my solicitor."

Jewle smiled. "Mr. Templett, you know better than that. If you've nothing to conceal, then you'll be back here in no time. All the same I think we shall have to send your receptionist home."

He gave me a nod. I went back to the reception room. I don't think she believed me when I said that Mr. Templett would be away for some days and she'd be notified about his return. She was almost crying when she gave me her name and address.

As soon as she'd gone, Jewle's two men came in. I went through to the office again. All the fight had gone from Templett. Jewle was holding his keys. A couple of minutes and we had that room to ourselves.

Jewle looked round. "A nice place, as you told him. He must have been making money."

It made Tom Jordan's office and my own look like a couple of rather moth-eaten Edwardian survivals. It had everything except an electronic computer.

"Might as well see what's in the filing cabinets," Jewle said. "You go through his desk."

It was a modern knee-hole desk of inlaid mahogany. Four of the five drawers were unlocked. There was nothing in them but an assortment of office stationery, a couple of staplers and the timesheets of the two operatives. Jewle gave me the keys and I opened the locked drawer. In it was a ledger, a cheque book, bank statements and half-a-dozen used cheque books. I put them on the desk. It was a bottom drawer and I ran my fingers around it in case there should be anything else.

There was: a small memorandum book with a black leather cover. About three inches by five. In its back was a thin pencil with a neat knob to keep it from slipping through.

I opened the book. What it was I couldn't make out. The entries looked like a kind of gibberish and far too elaborate for code. The first entry was dated Friday the 4th of October. I turned over a couple of pages. The gibberish continued.

Jewle was asking how I was getting along. I don't quite know why, but I slipped the little book into my pocket.

"I think these are all the files," he said. "Just about thirty. Would you call that a reasonable amount of business?"

I said it depended on the class of business he undertook and, maybe, on how much he spent on advertising.

"Right," he said. "Let's just have a general look round. Matthews can comb the place through later."

We found nothing else. We had a quick look through the secretary's desk.

"Right," Jewle said again. "We'll just tie everything up and leave it for Matthews to collect. I'd like to get back for a chat with Cofield. I have an idea he's the weak link."

He locked the door after us and made for the lift.

"Wonder if I could leave you for a bit," I said. "I just thought of something important I ought to do. I oughtn't to be more than an hour."

I don't know how the idea had come to me. Maybe it was simply the realisation that the little black book was a sort of diary. In the taxi I tried to make sense out of that gibberish again but again I got nowhere. In any case it was only a short drive to Whitney Street.

Just along it is the firm of Neddler & Co., Silversmiths, one of the best known firms in town. I knew Henry Neddler, and I was hoping he'd be in. He was.

He's a man of my own age, eminently likeable and the sort you feel you can trust. In his office we had a few friendly words and then he was asking what he could do for me. I said I was there on a highly confidential matter.

"Naturally you knew Stephen Daunt?"

"Of course," he said. "One way and another I've known him for years. A very nasty business that sudden death of his."

"It may be nastier than you think," I said. "My firm is assisting the police. This morning we came into possession of what may be his diary. Just a few memoranda he used to jot down every night before he went to sleep. To me they're just gibberish, so what I'd like you to do is to knock some sense into them."

I opened the book at a casual page. "Take this line for instance. What could it mean? Let's write it down."

The date was October the 15th. I said we had to keep in mind the fact that, if the book was really Daunt's, we were trying to decipher the memoranda of a silversmith like himself.

"Detective work's out of my line," he said, "but let's see what we can make of it."

S. s/g wcs P.S. £1500? Col G?

That was the line. He pursed his lips and frowned. "Looks as if he was wondering about a sum of money. Wait a minute, though. I have an idea."

From a filing cabinet he produced half-a-dozen sale catalogues. "Let's try these. It's just possible the S might stand for Sotheby's. What'd you say the date was?"

"October the 15th."

He selected a catalogue and began looking it through. He peered at the line again. A couple of minutes later we knew we had most of it. Sotheby's had had a silver sale on the 16th. A pair of silver-gilt wine-coolers by Paul Storr had made £1,800. Daunt had made up his mind to bid up to £1,500.

"And the Col. G.?"

"Don't know," he said. "Col may be Colonel. Might be a client he had in mind if he purchased."

"Mind if I use your phone?"

He told me to go ahead. I looked up Bendale's number and rang him. I said I was in a hurry and would explain later, but had his firm a client: a Colonel with a name beginning with G.?

"Oh, yes," he said. "An American collector named Grainger."

I thanked him hurriedly and rang off. I think I must have beamed at Henry Neddler.

"That makes this book Stephen Daunt's," I said. "That's what I hoped you'd be able to verify."

"You think we ought to try another entry or two?"

I laughed. "You've been bitten by the detection bug."

He laughed too. Maybe I was right. I put the book back in my pocket, thanked him warmly and left.

It's a longer ride from Whitney Street to the Yard. I had plenty of time to have a good look at that book. As I began checking I couldn't help noticing certain regularities but it was as I neared the end that I was suddenly aware of one vital thing. When I came to the final entry, I thought I knew the whole twisted workings of Daunt's mind.

Jewle was in. He said he'd only just ended his preliminary talk with Cofield. He'd sent him off to cool his heels in case he might want to add some more before making an official statement. I asked what Jewle had actually learned.

"Those women just made a tool of him, right from the word go," he said. "This is what actually happened when you piece it all together. When old John Parwell was taken ill, Caroline Daunt came back from Edinburgh to nurse him. She probably did a bit of foraging around while the old man was in bed and she found those replicas. When Morton Crewe no longer had any use for them he probably gave them to Parwell to keep and, since it'd all been a bit hush-hush, Parwell hadn't wanted to keep them in the office safe. Parwell must have told her the whole story.

"Then Lady Crewe died and at practically the same time as Parwell: say a few days later. There was a lot of publicity which gave Caroline ideas. She got the Vaile woman to go to Pentlow House and do some ferreting around. Vaile immediately got pally with Cofield and she passed him on to Caroline. Cofield fell for the scheme since all he had to do was induce Mrs. Crewe to take the jewels to Saffron Row at a certain date and time. The rest was up to Caroline. Cofield swears he didn't even know anything had happened till Mrs. Crewe told him he was wanted with herself at Lombard Street. He didn't even know it'd been a switch and not a theft till he was actually in Hill's office that morning. He also claims the women later told him it'd be safer if they kept the jewels till they were disposed of, and then he'd get his agreed cut: three thousand."

"He'd no idea how the switch was made?"

"Never an idea. I gather there was a whole lot of telephoning and questions, but he was always fobbed off, even when he went to Vaile's place to try to induce her to sell at least something so that he could pay off the blackmailer. He must have been properly scared." He gave a little grimace. "As to how the switch was worked, damned if I have the faintest idea either."

I brought out the little black book and told him where I'd found it. I told him what Neddler and I had found out. His eyes narrowed a bit.

"Daunt's diary. And found in Templett's possession. That places him right on the spot for the Daunt killing."

I said he'd probably kept it because he'd been intrigued, as I had, by the gibberish. Maybe he thought there might be something profitable in it.

"But look at this," I said, "and follow me carefully. Daunt began this book as soon as he took over at Saffron Row. He may have used one in Edinburgh. I don't know, but he was making a new start with a new book, and we're all what they call creatures of habit. You can check later, but you'll find there was an entry of sorts for every night except Saturdays. On Saturdays he wouldn't have to remind himself of the next day's plans. Then the Sundays. There's always an entry on Sundays, but not for one particular Sunday—Sunday November the 3rd. Look at it."

S/d Bate . . .

That was all. The last three letters trailed slightly downwards and ended in a tiny scrawl.

"You see?" I said. "He began to write but he didn't finish it. I think I know why. It was because his wife had heavily doped his toddy. No sooner was he putting pencil to paper than he was falling asleep."

"Yes," he said slowly. "It could be just that. She helped herself to his keys and took the replicas to Saffron Row. If she went by Tube she could have been back in under an hour. Cofield admitted he rang her on the Saturday before lunch and told her where the jewellery'd been put."

"That's it," I said. "It couldn't be anything else. No Houdini business. No gentleman hired from the Magic Circle: just a simple case of doping."

"Wait a moment," he said. "When Daunt woke in the morning he must have guessed something had happened the previous night."

"If he did," I said, "he couldn't explain it. He probably put it down to some sort of indisposition, especially as his wife was there to agree. But that was before he got to his office that Monday morning. That's when I'm pretty sure he began to think. Take another look at the book."

After that beginning of an entry on the night of Sunday, November the 3rd, there wasn't an entry of any kind. Except one. It was on the following page and what was written was in capitals.

SINCE YOU'RE READING THIS
YOU KNOW THAT I KNOW.

"You see?" I said. "He suspected. He made the book a kind of trap. He probably left the book lying around, and all the time he'd be watching her every word and action to see if she'd fallen into it. My guess is that the book just didn't interest her. It had no significance."

Except as a nail in the Templetts' coffins for the Daunt killing, that book, as Jewle said, mightn't have to be used at all. But it did show something of the state of Daunt's mind in the days that followed the discovery of the substitutes. There'd also been that matter of a denial that I'd seen his wife in Regent Street.

No wonder Daunt had fallen clean into Geoff Templett's lap when he learned that his wife was having an affair with Cofield.

16
ROUNDING IT OFF

THERE seems to be a general idea that the police have a habit of playing off one suspect against another. It just isn't true. I know from experience. And I've looked it up.

In para. 8 of the memorandum approved by His Majesty's (1912) Judges of the King's Bench Division concerning statements by persons suspected of crime, or by prisoners in police custody, it is expressly laid down that the police have no right to invite one co-defendant or suspect to make a statement against another and that a conviction obtained by such improper means cannot be upheld. In the case of the Templetts there'd been no need for any disregard of that ruling, even if Jewle had been the sort to risk it. Which he wasn't.

Fred Templett was the one who talked. The police had more on him in any case. What was interesting was his account of what had happened that Sunday night at Hollindale.

His car had been drawn into the Southways drive to avoid identification and to act as a block when Cofield later made a bolt from the house. Geoff had done the talking and Daunt had moved along the grass verge to listen. All that evening, Fred said, he'd been very edgy. When Geoff came back to wait in the car, Daunt was following him. He said Geoff had had no right to mention his name and do what he'd done. What he'd thought was that there'd have been a knock at the front door and then the Templetts would have entered when Cofield opened it and he'd follow on himself. That was what had been arranged.

He'd been furious about the change. Also he was talking too loudly. Geoff told him fiercely to shut up. Daunt seized him by the arm and Geoff threw him as furiously away. That's how he came to fall against the hub-cap of the car.

Geoff Templett got six years and Fred seven. I thought it a miscarriage of justice that it hadn't been the other way about. With regard to the jewellery business, there was a lot of skirmishing behind the scenes. Scandal or no scandal, someone had to bring a charge. Hill might have been satisfied with the recovery of the jewellery, but it was Julia Crewe—the stem old Roman matron—who, so I gathered, had insisted on the whole thing being brought to light. This time justice was impartial. It was Vaile who broke and she and Daunt each got two years. As for Cofield, I think it was David Crewe who threw him, so to speak, to the wolves. He got a couple of years too.

I didn't go to Pentlow House again, but before the Crewes left for Kenya they asked me to see them. I pleaded pressure of business. That was over the telephone. Later Julia wrote expressing the wish to recompense me in some way for what I'd done. I thanked her and said that we'd been well rewarded already.

Pentlow House was sold just after the Crewes left. I wished I'd had the money, and the leisure, to buy it myself: at least that's what I thought in some romantic moment at the time. Ludovic Travers, squire of Newhurst; tramping the countryside in hob-nailed boots and deer-stalker hat. A few days and it wasn't so attractive. By the way, I hadn't mentioned those ambitions to Bernice. I never did.

The Crewe jewellery comes up for sale next week and I'd like to be there. Hill tells me it might make as much as sixty thousand: quite a nice haul for the Crewes. Even after tax Julia ought to be able to refurbish pretty handsomely that farm of theirs. There might be enough left over for a friendly gesture; the presentation, say, of a gold-plated fly-whisk to Jomo Kenyatta. But the Crewes were nice people. They've made me sometimes wonder what it'd be like living in Kenya myself.

One other thing. The other day in the course of a conversation with Jewle, he asked me if I'd ever deciphered that entry Daunt had made that Sunday night as the dope began taking hold of him. I thought it was an occasion to spread myself a bit and said that I had. He didn't see through the show of modesty and I think he really thought I was someone. As a matter of fact, it had been easy. The date, Sunday, November the 3rd, meant an anticipation of something on the Monday. I looked up my own priced catalogues and ran it down. Among the items to be sold on the Monday at Christie's was a strawberry dish by the Batemans.

How did the Broad Street Detective Agency come out of it all? Pretty well on the whole. We got our bonus on only the insured value, plus, of course, time and expenses. Five per-cent on forty-eight thousand isn't a fortune but it's not a bankruptcy notice either. Mind you, we felt like handing out a bonus or two ourselves: just something by way of thanks to Robert Lockyer and the Frodens.

When you get mixed up, as I'm always doing, with people like the Caroline Daunts and Vailes and Cofields and Templetts, you're apt to talk too glibly about the loss of spiritual values and of faith in human nature. You forget the Lockyers, the Frodens, the Crewes, the Caplins and the Rawsons: the kindly, reliable, likeable people who'll always be the salt of the earth.

Which reminds me. Prolixity is one of the infirmities of advancing years and I've just remembered that I've more or less said all that before. Not that I mightn't devote a little more attention to the philosophy business. It can bring in dividends. At the worst it might be something to think about for when some day the time comes to retire.

THE END

www.ingramcontent.com/pod-product-compliance
Lightning Source LLC
Chambersburg PA
CBHW030757190726
48285CB00003B/901